DANNI'S
DESPERATE
JOURNEY

DANNI'S DESPERATE JOURNEY

Ann Grocott

ANGUS
& ROBERTSON
PUBLISHERS

For the original Danni

Creative writing programme assisted by the
Literature Board of the Australia Council,
the Federal Government's arts funding
and advisory body.

ANGUS & ROBERTSON PUBLISHERS

Unit 4, Eden Park, 31 Waterloo Road,
North Ryde, NSW, Australia 2113, and
16 Golden Square, London WIR 4BN,
United Kingdom

First published in Australia
by Angus & Robertson Publishers in 1987
First published in the United Kingdom
by Angus & Robertson (UK) in 1987

Copyright © Ann Grocott, 1987

Grocott, Ann.
   Danni's desperate journey.

   ISBN 0 207 15568 2.

   I. Title.

A823'.3

Typeset in 12/13 Paladium by Midland Typesetters
Printed in Australia by Australian Print Group

CONTENTS

1

DANGER
IN THE DUCKPEN

The egg was as big as a giant's football. It was covered in slippery, slimy, greeny-grey mould, which dripped over it like treacle. In the mould, strange toad-coloured fungus flowers grew as healthily and happily as the sweet peas in Danni's garden.

Danni squatted in the muddy shadows next to the duckpond and stared at the egg. "How did you get here?" she asked. "None of my ducks laid you, that's for sure!"

The egg made no reply. It smelled of dirty gutters.

Danni stood up and stalked around it, holding her nose. No matter how hard she pinched her nostrils, the smell crept in and lurked like a prowling stranger. It got on her nerves. She poked irritably at the egg with her rake. "Who brought you here? You weren't asked to come. Why don't you get out?"

The egg remained exactly where it was. The fungus flowers seemed to smirk and jeer at her.

"I said, *get out!*" repeated Danni unreasonably. Her head was swimming. She coughed. "You're making me sick!"

The egg did not budge.

"All right! You asked for it!" Making a short run through the mud, Danni punted the stinking egg with her sandal. The egg made a hollow, popping sound and broke in two. Inside was a jungle-coloured custardy yolk. It dribbled onto the mud, which sucked it up with greedy, lip-smacking noises.

A wormy something had stuck to Danni's big toe. A thin, wiggly squiggle of slime. Danni shook her foot but it wouldn't come off. She grabbed a frond of the bamboo which grew in a corner of the duckpen and wiped it off on that. By this time, the custardy yolk had been completely swallowed up by the mud. The glistening mould on the shattered shell was drying to wispy hairs, and the once-proud fungus flowers were drooping sadly.

Danni bit her lip. Even the terrible stink was fading. The egg had died so quickly – and she had been the cause of it. How could she have lost her head and destroyed the remarkable egg? "I'm sorry," she whispered. "It must have been your smell. You drove me mad!"

Even in halves, the egg was enormous. Danni wondered what sort of creature could lay something so big. She glanced nervously around the duckpen. "I hope your mother doesn't turn up!"

As Danni spoke, the duckpond heaved. Five ducks swimming on it suddenly became feathery balls. A tidal wave tossed them to the banks of the pond. Danni spun away from the egg and her mouth dropped open as something unknown, something immense, rose from the depths of her duckpond.

First came a huge, blackish-green, scaly head. It had a pointy snout and fringed double eyelids over hidden eyes. Second came a long snaky neck, followed by pointed shoulders with short arms and flipper-like hands. Next came a round, leathery body with a bulging barrel belly and loose, roomy pouch. A few seconds later, two powerful stumpy legs with gigantic, six-toed feet landed *bam-splat!* one after the other on the edge of the pond. Last to emerge was a thick, blunt tail, which slapped at the ground raising showers of mud.

And that wasn't all. Two dripping wings as big as king-size sheets unfurled from behind the creature's back and totally blocked out the sunlight. The creature was as high as a house, and as wide as an elephant. Water cascaded down its ballooning wings, drenching Danni's scarlet shirt and cream towelling shorts and making spikes of her shaggy brown hair so that she looked like a startled dish mop.

Chucha, chucha, chucha, went Danni's teeth. She felt her lips turn to iceblocks, her legs turn to wood.

The creature bent.

Danni couldn't move . . . she waited to be squashed like a bug.

She may as well have been a bug, for all the creature's attention was given to the broken egg. Tenderly, its pointy snout sniffled and snuffled backwards and forwards over the shattered pieces.

For what seemed like ages, the creature gently swayed from side to side, caressing the egg with its snout until amber tears spurted from under its double eyelids and, very slowly, it straightened up.

Boom, boom, the creature beat its chest like a mighty drum. "Whoo, whoo, whoo," it wailed, in a grief-stricken, heart-broken way. "Whoo, whoo, whoo."

Lost in the terrible wail, Danni almost forgot how terrified she was. Some feeling crept back to her body. Her legs began to shake. "S . . . so th . . . that was y . . . y . . . your egg?" she stammered. "I'm v . . . very s . . . sorry I broke it. I d . . . didn't think it would matter." Her knees gave way and she collapsed in the mud.

"Whoo, whoo, whoo, whoo." Shifting from one six-toed foot to the other, the creature swayed in time with each *boom, boom* on its chest.

Truly sorry for being the cause of so much sorrow, Danni crept out from the creature's shadow. On all fours, she slithered to the gate of the duckpen, making long channels through the mud. Safely outside, with the gate fastened, she watched the grieving monster through the wire netting. At last its wailing and chest-beating ceased. The creature bent again and, shovelling mud with its flippers, covered the broken egg and stamped it flat with a thump of one foot. Then it turned. This wasn't easy, for its great body took up almost the entire pen. Snout pointed towards Danni, the creature blinked.

Danni caught a fleeting glimpse of eyes clear as ice and green as spring lettuce. The snout remained trained on her, straight as a rifle barrel. Dark green nostrils wrinkled and flared. *Snuffle, snuffle.* The snout eased towards her, snuffling and bubbling like a dentist's sucker.

Snuffle, snuffle. The creature's neck grew longer and snakier. The snout came closer.

Danni stepped back a pace.

The snout came over the top of the netting.

Danni stepped back another pace.

Snuffle, bubble, sniff, snuffle. The snout was much too close. Danni could see right down the quivering nostrils.

She turned and ran.

Ccrraaarrk! Danni stopped. What a strange sound! She couldn't resist glancing over her shoulder. Her brown eyes grew round and shiny. The creature couldn't be smiling!

But it was. Long, long, elastic jaws were stretched into a lizardy grin. "Mimi, mimi," it trilled. "Mimi, mimi, mi mi mi mi mimi!"

Danni giggled, and skipped back to the fence. "Actually, I'm not Mimi," she said. "I'm Danni. Are you happy at last? Could you lay another egg and forget about the one I broke?"

"Mimi, mi mi mi mimi." The creature chuckled and wiggled its flippers deliciously.

"Danni, *not* Mimi," corrected Danni. She leaned her head to one side. "Perhaps Mimi is your name? You don't look like a Mimi though. You look more like . . . um . . ."

Wagging its head foolishly, the creature trilled and

mimi-ed over and over again.

"Stay there!" ordered Danni. "I'll fetch Mum. She'll take photos of you smiling for the paper. You'll be famous."

The creature stopped chuckling. It stopped trilling. It stamped its feet instead. *Ker-ash! Ker-ash!* A clawed flipper shot over the wire fence and grabbed the collar of Danni's shirt.

"Hey!" protested Danni. "I'm only going to get Mum. I won't be away for long."

Down swept the sniffling, snuffling snout. Before Danni could draw a breath, the creature wrapped both flippers about her waist and lifted her up and over the wire netting.

"What are you doing? You stupid . . .!" Danni's nose was pressed flat against a rock-hard chest which smelled of compost.

"Mimi, mimi, mi mi mimi," sang the creature, pushing Danni downwards. The pouch yawned open like a monstrous mouth.

"No! No!" yelled Danni, butting with her head. "Stop it! Stop! *Let me go!*" She kicked out as hard as she could. She wriggled and squirmed until she faced away from the scaly chest. She hammered and battered at the creature's arms with her fists. "LET ME GO! *Help, Mum! Help, anybody! Help! Help!*"

The creature chuckled as it managed to push one of Danni's feet into its pouch.

"YERK!" The pouch felt as moist as a tongue. It felt enfolding and clinging and horribly warm. Danni's foot leapt out as if scalded. She was yelling herself hoarse. "*Help! Help! Help!*"

The clumps of bamboo unexpectedly whispered together. The noise distracted the creature and it craned its neck upward, snout to the sky, as if listening with its nose.

Danni kept struggling. Puffing, panting, tearing at scales, she tried to prise apart the creature's arms, but they remained firmly locked about her. She pressed back into the creature's mulchy chest and tried to squirm under the arms instead.

It was then she caught a glint of gold. For a moment, Danni stopped squirming. Whoever was that?

A strange young man was standing outside her duckpen. Very strange, she thought. He doesn't have ordinary feet — he's got webs, just like those on my ducks but much bigger. At least he doesn't look scary.

She yelled to him: "This thing wants to put me in its pouch — but I don't want to go in there!"

The stranger smiled up at her. He had the whitest teeth, the straightest nose and the clearest grey eyes Danni had ever seen. The sheen of gold she'd glimpsed was sunlight shining on his long, golden hair.

"I'm not surprised you object to going into a Moldy Flizzard's pouch," he said pleasantly. "I can't imagine why it wants to put you in there either."

"Can't you do something?" pleaded Danni. "See, it's doing it again!" And her legs went *whack, whack, whack*, against the creature's belly.

The young man's arms and legs were bare and he wore an odd black garment, like a tube with rows and rows of pockets up and down it. Why doesn't he stop patting those pockets and help me? thought Danni, struggling and straining as hard as she could. "Please," she gasped, "can't you get me away from this . . . what did you call it? Moldy Flizzard?"

"Sure." The man opened pocket after pocket, exploring the contents with long fingers. "But I can't remember which pocket I need."

"Hurry!" begged Danni. "I'm getting so tired, and I'll die if it puts me in that pouch. I know I will!"

"Ah! Here it is." He drew out a folding umbrella of gentian blue, poked the sharp end through the wire netting and jabbed it smartly into the Flizzard's left knee.

In an instant Danni was dropped and in less than an

instant she was off. Legs churning like eggbeaters, she burst out of the pen while the Moldy Flizzard was still clutching its knee.

The young man took her hand. "Moldy Flizzards' weak spots are their knees," he explained as they fled from the duckpen.

Behind a clump of snowy lilies, they flattened themselves to the ground. "It won't find you here," said the man confidently. "Moldy Flizzards have extremely poor eyesight."

"Phew!" sighed Danni. "Thanks for rescuing me. There surely couldn't be anything worse than going into a Moldy Flizzard's pouch!"

Her rescuer frowned. "Usually only eggs go in their pouches. Each egg has a distinctive smell of its own and . . ."

A roar of thunder came from the duckpen. The roar was followed by the sound of splintering wood. Peeping through lily leaves, Danni saw the Moldy Flizzard smashing her duckpen gate to smithereens. Worse than that, poor eyesight or not, it appeared to know *exactly* where she was. The snuffling snout was unmistakeably pointed in her direction.

The creature would reach her in one easy step.

2

A HORRIBLE POSSIBILITY

"It's coming! It's coming!" yelled Danni.

To her horror, the young man just stood up and calmly stowed the umbrella away in a pocket. "Take hold of the loops on my back," he said, turning to show Danni two long loops hanging from the shoulders of his black tube.

"Why?" Danni asked.

"Do as I say." He began to breathe very deeply, in and out, in and out.

The ground trembled around them. Crisp white lilies and waxy green leaves crackled and sighed under a heedless great foot. The Moldy Flizzard had taken its one step. Its scaly face went *Ccrraaarrrkk* into another smile. It reached for Danni.

Danni bounded to her feet and grabbed the shoulder loops. An instant later, her feet left the ground as both she and the young man rose into the air. A disappointed bellow nearly blasted her ears away, but she had missed the clutches of the Moldy Flizzard by a flea's whisker. Grimly, she clung to the loops, wondering what was going on. When first she tried to speak, she could only manage two or three sobbing sounds.

Who would believe it? So this is how he got to my duckpen. This man with the webs can fly! It's crazy, but it's real!

The young man continued his steady, deep breathing. His arms were stretched out as if they rested on comfortable cushions of air and his long hair trailed behind like a golden banner.

For a few moments, Danni forgot the Moldy Flizzard. Always, she had wanted to fly — to cruise over mountaintops, to plummet as a sea-eagle after fish, to skim over ocean waves. She laughed, and the wind snatched her chuckles, puffing her cheeks into little balloons.

Way beneath her, the ground looked like a movie on fast forward. Trees, houses, cars and roads reeled away so fast it made her dizzy to look. Danni thought how surprised someone would be to look up and see the two of them flying without wings.

"Wings!" she cried as she suddenly remembered. "The Moldy Flizzard's got wings! Great big flappy ones. Won't it follow us?"

The man's breathing became quicker and deeper. They travelled faster, so fast the scenery below turned into a blur.

After a time, they suddenly veered right and slowed down. The man's breathing changed to short, sharp gasps. For a moment he seemed to hover in the air, before floating earthward, webs first.

As her feet touched ground, Danni dropped the loops and looked around. They were high in pine-covered mountains with not a sign of civilisation. The air was fresh and fragrant. She turned to gaze at the person who had come into her life as abruptly as had the Moldy Flizzard. "Who are you?" she asked bluntly, trying not to stare at his amazing webs. "Where do you come from and what are you doing here?"

He laughed. A tinkling, musical, up and down laugh which made Danni smile. "I suppose it was a bit of a surprise having me turn up like that. I heard you calling for help. My name is Kroninkliwzotl and I don't come from Earth. My planet is called Lex and the reason I'm here is to try out some new Mos tablets for NITT."

"Nit?"

"New Ideas Testing Team. I belong to the team and we have to try out all sorts of new products in lots of different places."

Danni nodded, attempting to look wise but feeling bewildered. "I'm Danni and I'm very glad you heard me. Does the Moldy Flizzard come from Lex, Kro . . . er . . . Krokl . . . um . . . Kroning . . .?"

"Kroninkliwzotl. It's hard to say, isn't it? You could think of something easier to call me, if you like."

"How about Webbers?" blurted Danni. She chewed her lip in shame—she couldn't keep her mind off those webs.

But her companion only laughed merrily. "That's a good, practical name for me." He shook her hand. "Pleased to meet you, Danni. Glad I could help you. Now, about Moldy Flizzards. They don't come from Lex; they come from a very swampy place called Zubel. Normally they don't travel far, for Zubel has everything they need—lots of water, all the grasses they can eat and plenty of peace and quiet. Lately, however, there have been some new arrivals on Zubel, the Simbans, who've been draining the swamps, depriving the Flizzards of much of their natural habitat and disturbing their peace. Some Moldy Flizzards have left Zubel to look for new, quieter homes suitable for raising their young, which hatch out of eggs kept in their pouches."

"So the Moldy Flizzard in my duckpen arrived on Earth looking for a peaceful place to hatch its egg?"

"Probably. They lay only one egg in their whole lifetime and think only of caring for it. Each egg is covered in mould and has a unique smell which the mother gives it."

"It's a terrible smell!" said Danni, screwing up her nose at the memory.

"Not to the mother—to her, it's sweeter than honeysuckle. It means the joy of her life's work. There is no mother more caring, more loving than a Moldy Flizzard mother. Wait!" Webbers paused. Frowned. "How do you know the egg has a terrible smell?"

"Because I found one. I feel awful about breaking that egg," admitted Danni. "You see, it stank, and it looked so strange with all that slippery mould and those funny-looking flowers growing all over it-t-t-t-"

Webbers was shaking her like a rattle. "You broke a Flizzard's egg? How did you break the egg? You didn't touch it, did you? No! You couldn't have touched it! Nobody would touch a Moldy Flizzard's egg!"

Danni stared at him. A little shiver skipped up her spine. "The egg was on the ground all alone while the Flizzard was in the duckpond," she squeaked. "I didn't actually touch it — I kicked it. I'm terribly sorry about it, Webbers. I can't think why the smell made me so mad . . ."

Webbers' voice cracked in the clear air. "If a Moldy Flizzard's egg touches skin — or even just brushes it — mould will grow on that spot. The mould continues to grow until it covers the body completely. Such an unfortunate body would turn into a kind of walking Flizzard's egg!"

Every bit of colour drained from Danni's face. Her stomach churned. "I k . . . kicked it. Some slime got on my toe but I wiped it off quickly." She saw a nightmarish picture of herself covered in mould and fungus flowers, smelling of slimy gutters, just like the departed egg.

Lips set in a grim line, Webbers groaned. "I'll have to examine your toe. If there's even a speck of mould there, the situation is bad." His face grew even more troubled. "That Flizzard seemed to smell you, Danni. Their eyesight is poor but their sense of smell is superior to that of any creature I know. If you bear the scent of its beloved egg, it will follow you forever!"

A lump sat in Danni's throat. She couldn't swallow. Her teeth started clacking together. The shiver turned into an icy spear up her backbone and her stomach tightened into a ball. "C . . . can you do any . . . anything to save me?" she croaked.

"Take off your sandal. I'll look at your toe."

Sitting on the pine needles, Danni tried to undo the buckles on her muddy red sandal, with her fingers trembling so much it took three attempts to take it off. "That's the toe," she said, pointing at the grubby big toe on her right foot.

Careful not to touch it, Webbers bent and examined the toe intently. "I can't see anything. But that doesn't mean the mould isn't there. The Moldy Flizzard picked you up."

"And d . . . definitely wanted me in its pouch." Danni shuddered, remembering the warm, sucking, wet feeling on her foot. She imagined the pouch closing over her head and almost screamed.

"Find a cure for the mould," mumbled Webbers, standing up. "That's the only thing to do."

"Is there a cure?"

"I don't know, but I'll try to find one. It means you'll have to leave Earth for a time, Danni. I have many friends and someone may know of a cure. We'll have to move fast. Even a speck of mould grows so quickly it can cover your body in a matter of days."

Danni felt helpless and miserably wronged. It was unfair. "Why did that *stupid* Flizzard leave its *stupid* egg on the ground? Why didn't it take the egg with it into the pond?"

"The Moldy Flizzard travelled a long and tiring way to get to Earth," explained Webbers. "Its scales would have dried out after such a long journey. You can be sure it needed to soak in the water for a long time. Eggs are never soaked because the mould and fungus flowers, which act as protection, might be damaged."

"It *would* have to leave its egg there just as I went down to the duckpond, wouldn't it?" cried Danni angrily. "And why pick on *my* duckpen, anyway? It's not fair!"

"I don't suppose the Moldy Flizzard thought it fair that someone broke its beloved egg," said Webbers, taking a silver comb and a scrolled oval mirror from a pocket, "and I don't suppose it thought it fair that its substitute egg — you — was whisked away from under its snout." He combed his golden hair until it sparkled. He checked his face in the mirror, running his fingers delicately over his high cheekbones. "Anyway, talking will get us nowhere. The Flizzard could turn up at any minute. If there's a mould on your toe, traces of smell are probably all over the atmosphere, even if we can't smell anything ourselves."

Danni wiggled her bare toe. It seemed so innocent. There wasn't a sign of anything unusual on it, apart from dried mud. She hadn't thought much about her toe before but now that she knew it to be in great danger she gazed at it lovingly. Never in her life had she felt so fond of her toe. "How will I explain this to Mum, Webbers? She won't believe a word of it."

Webbers smiled. "We don't need to worry your mother unless we fail to find a cure, and I don't want to think about that. We'll be travelling so fast, we'll store up time credits. With luck, you won't be away long enough — in Earth-time — to be missed."

Danni shivered. It's ridiculous, she thought, but I have no choice. I have to trust Webbers. Swallowing the lump in her throat at last, she buckled on her sandal and stood up. "I'm ready to go."

"Good girl!" Webbers squeezed her hand. "We'll visit the Grablet first. It's always boasting about how much it knows — perhaps it can help us. There's also a NITT experiment I left on the Grablet's planet which may provide food for you."

Her stomach was still in very bad shape. Danni was sure she'd never feel hungry again, but she didn't say so.

Webbers searched his pockets. He turned out a slim pencil, three boxes of coloured matches, a faded sunflower, an unopened paper package, a pair of nail clippers and a dog-eared book with a biscuit-coloured cover before he found what he wanted. It was a square, flattish bottle with a glass stopper and contained hundreds of tiny balls in different colours. "These are the Mos tablets I'm testing and the reason I visited Earth today. The tablets allow people to breathe in different atmospheres so we don't have to wear helmets any more. Always hated helmets — they upset the hair so much. These Mos tablets have been fine, so far." Shaking out two yellow tablets, he swallowed one and held the other out to Danni.

Danni closed her eyes and opened her mouth.

"The yellows have been fully tested for space," explained Webbers, placing the yellow tablet on her tongue.

After swallowing it, Danni waited a second and said, "I don't feel any different."

"You won't. It just means you can breathe in space." Webbers crammed everything back into his pockets and began taking his deep, deep breaths. "Hold onto my loops . . . *puff* . . . like you did before . . . *puff* . . . Danni. We're off!"

As Danni wound the loops about her wrists, she whispered, "Goodbye for now, my Earth. I hope I'll be back soon, without nasty mould all over my body."

Under the scarlet shirt, her heart pounded like a jackhammer, but not only with fear. It was beating out a song of excitement at starting the greatest adventure of her life.

3

GREETING THE GRABLET

They left Earth behind. The first time Danni looked back she saw mountains, fields and towns spread out like an ever-shrinking map; the second time, she saw jigsaw shapes of cloud-streaked land swimming in a vast ocean. The third time, all she saw was a pretty blue ball.

The wind was no longer rushing past her ears. It was still and black, for they had left the Earth's atmosphere behind and were now in space. Danni had never felt so small. Smaller than the smallest speck of dust. She was glad she wasn't alone.

For quite a time they travelled, but there was little to see, only the twinkle of distant stars, and so Danni slept. She was woken by Webbers, who reached over his shoulder and tapped her on the head. "You have to take a purple Mos before we land," he said, holding out the tiny tablet between thumb and forefinger.

Danni yawned. "Are we there already?" She unwound a loop from one wrist and took the Mos tablet. "That big planet ahead of us, is that where we're going? It looks very dark, not blue and sparkling like Earth."

"That's the Grablet's homeland. It receives only a feeble light from a faraway sun." Webbers' deep breathing changed to short gasps, and their speed slackened. "Don't forget to tell me if you feel sick or dizzy, or strange in any

15

way. Not all the Mos tablets have been fully tested."

"Okay, but I feel fine so far," said Danni. "I'm looking forward to meeting this Grablet."

When they landed, she wondered how anyone could possibly live in such a barren, cold and uninviting place. It consisted of bare, craggy rocks jutting out of stony ground, with no sign of grass or anything in the least bit comforting. An icy wind whistled around the crags and the whole place was bathed in a gloomy half-light, like a wintry evening on Earth. Danni blew on her chilled fingers and stamped her numb feet. "Are you sure you've come to the right place?" she asked.

"Of course I'm sure." Webbers finally found a torch after searching six pockets. "I've been here many times before." He flashed the torch under some rocks and called out: "Ho there, Grablet! Where are you?"

Danni thought it odd that Webbers was looking under rocks for his friend. She listened for the Grablet's reply but heard only the wind howling a bleak, forsaken tune.

"Grablet! It's important I talk to you. Please answer me!"

Danni wished a friendly someone would suddenly appear, ask her into a cosy room and give her hot cocoa and crumpets. Her appetite had returned after all. "Hasn't the Grablet got a house?" she asked.

"No. It lives out here among the rocks and listens to the voices in the wind."

"This Grablet must be a nutcase," muttered Danni, jogging up and down and slapping her thighs to keep warm.

"Ouch! Watch what you're doing, you great galumphing idiot!" shouted a testy voice. "And I am *not* a nutcase! Do you hear me? I am *not a nutcase!*"

Danni sprang backwards. "What's that? Webbers! Something talked under my foot!"

"Sounds like the Grablet." Webbers swept torchlight over the stony ground. "Yes! Here's my little friend." He picked up a fist-sized object and held it out for Danni to see. The object gave off a dull glow in the half-light and Danni stepped closer for a better look.

It was unimpressive. Just a lump of something with a number of holes dotted here and there. Some of the holes were squeezing themselves into slits. Danni hadn't expected the Grablet to be so small and uninteresting.

"How are you, Grablet?" asked Webbers. "I haven't seen you for a while."

The lump snorted. "Did you have to bring a horse with you? I do not appreciate being trampled on when I'm deep in meditation."

"I didn't mean to," apologised Danni. "I didn't know you'd be on the ground."

"My fault," said Webbers. "I should have explained. Anyway, Grablet, I brought Danni here because I hoped you could help her."

"And how could a nutcase help anyone?" sniffed the Grablet.

"Sorry," broke in Danni. "I didn't mean what I said. I didn't think anyone would hear me."

"That's no excuse!" snapped the Grablet.

"We appear to have started badly," said Webbers. "Let's begin again. I'll introduce you two properly and I'm sure you'll find each other very nice."

"We shall see," said the Grablet in a very snooty voice.

"Danni, meet the Grablet. A remarkable and interesting being."

But before Danni could say anything, the Grablet spoke. "Yes, indeed. I am most remarkable and very interesting. I am also extremely clever. One of a kind, you might say. My knowledge of poetry is endless and I can sing like an angel."

"How do you do?" replied Danni. "I don't know much poetry but I can sing too. In fact, I make up my own songs."

"Sounds amateurish," scoffed the Grablet.

"Grablet, meet Danni from Earth," said Webbers.

"Almost pleased to meet you . . . I think," said the Grablet ungraciously.

"Danni has a problem . . ."

"Big feet?" interrupted the Grablet, and cackled raucously.

"I don't think the Grablet wants to help," said Danni crossly. "Anyway, what could a little lump like that tell us?"

"You'd be surprised, Miss Earthgirl," said the Grablet.

"This is silly!" said Webbers. "Look, Grablet, Danni kicked a Moldy Flizzard's egg and she may have a mould on her toe."

"Good gracious! What a thoroughly stupid thing to do. Nobody in their right mind would touch a Moldy Flizzard's egg. And she called *me* a nutcase!"

"Do you know of a cure?" asked Webbers. "If you can't help we'll have to leave straight away. As you know, a Flizzard mould can completely cover someone's body in a very short time."

"That's not all," said the Grablet. "What about the mother of the egg? She'll smell that mould anywhere."

"Exactly," said Webbers. "That's why we can't waste any time."

"I don't want any Flizzards here," grumbled the Grablet, "ruining my peace, upsetting rocks all over the place."

"Do you know of a cure?" repeated Webbers.

"Let me think," replied the Grablet. "It's not a question one is asked very often. It needs some pondering. I do believe that several hundred years ago I heard mention of something regarding this. Some travellers from another place were here and we had a discussion about it."

"What did they say?"

"It was such a long time ago, but I should remember. If I can only think of a key to unlock the right train of thought. So much is crammed inside me, you know."

18

"If you can remember anything at all, it might help us," encouraged Webbers.

"Hurry, please, before I freeze to death," moaned Danni. "The mould won't have time to grow if I stay here much longer." Just then her stomach decided it wouldn't be ignored a moment longer and growled so loudly Webbers heard it above the whistle of the wind.

"You need food to warm you up," he said. "That reminds me — I left a NITT experiment here. How's the Inter-Planetary Piping Hot Pie Preserver going, Grablet?"

"How would I know? I've been in the same position ever since your last visit. I don't get up and move around except in emergencies and there haven't been any of those."

"I'll get it. You stay here with the Grablet, Danni." He handed the lump to her and disappeared from sight behind a towering rock.

Danni studied the Grablet. It felt cool and smooth on her hand, like the bottom of a glass. It was the colour of pewter and shaped like a bun. She counted seventeen holes. The holes were uneven, crimped around the edges. She turned the Grablet around and peeped through some of the holes.

"Well?" barked the Grablet, and a couple of holes elongated for a moment.

"You say you're clever," said Danni. "What can you do?"

"Anything, girl, anything," replied the Grablet smugly.

"Right! I'll have a cup of hot cocoa."

"Well, *almost* anything," said the Grablet.

"How about an insy-minsy bag of chips?"

"You can't expect miracles!" huffed the Grablet.

"You said you could do anything. You're a fraud," sneered Danni. "I bet you can't sing either!"

"*Sing!*" shouted the Grablet, and four of its holes squeezed together like buttonholes. "That's it! That's the key I was looking for!"

"What key? What do you mean?"

"A song, a song, a song," babbled the Grablet. "The cure was in a song. I remember now; at least, I think I do. After all these years . . . Those long-ago travellers — I can't remember who they were or where they came from, but I can remember them singing a cure. A cure for the mould from a Moldy Flizzard's egg. It was quite complicated."

"Is it like a spell? You say the words and the mould disappears?"

"No, not like that. The song tells of places to go to and things to get. When all the things are mixed together you have the cure."

"You might be clever after all, Grablet," said Danni. "How does the song go?"

"Hang on, girl, I think it's coming." The Grablet was silent for a minute. "Where a sun outshines . . . no . . . where a sun *outstrips*. That's it! Where a sun outstrips the rainbow, on a strange and distant star. Now what comes next?"

Just then, Webbers reappeared carrying a narrow white box. "Looks perfect on the outside," he said, setting the box on a ledge of rock. "Now let's see about the inside."

Danni leaned over, watching him unclip the top of the box. An irresistibly yummy smell wafted onto the chilly air, and her mouth watered. Two crusty pies sat in the box. Pies were among Danni's favourite food and wisps of steam rising from them proved they were piping hot.

Webbers looked happy. "They've been there about a year in your Earth-time, Danni. Not bad, eh? They still look as fresh as when they were put into the Preserver back on Lex."

Danni wanted to grab a pie and sink her teeth into it right then and there. She didn't know if just one would be enough. But what about Webbers and the Grablet? Would they be hungry too? She was saved any further worry when Webbers said "Have both of them. I don't eat, and neither does the Grablet."

"Waste of time," added the Grablet.

"You don't eat?" Danni's eyebrows nearly touched her hairline. "You mean you don't eat at all? Not ever?"

Webbers laughed. "Air is enough for me."

"Me too," said the Grablet.

"Well, I'm really glad it's not enough for me," said Danni. "I love eating." She picked up the first pie and took a bite. Delicious! Meat and peas, swimming in gravy, encased in feather-light pastry, met a great reception in her mouth. "Wonderful!" she mumbled.

"Seems the Inter-Planetary Piping Hot Pie Preserver is a success for NITT," said Webbers, jotting down a note about it on a chunky notepad.

Having finished the first pie, Danni started the second, a creamy rhubarb pie which she polished off with no trouble at all. She wiped her mouth and grinned. "I feel better now."

The white box, which had appeared so solid, was collapsing under Webbers' hands. He folded it up until it was no bigger than his notepad and tucked it in a pocket. "Good little gadget," he remarked.

"Webbers! The Grablet remembered a song about a cure for the mould," said Danni. "Isn't the Grablet clever?"

"What marvellous news! Grablet, you are the greatest!"

"Naturally," agreed the Grablet. "The song has a number of verses telling where to go to get certain items to mix up into a cure." It made a throat-clearing noise and sang in a high, wavering voice:

> *Where a sun outstrips the rainbow,*
> *On a strange and distant star,*
> *Take a dash of purple water,*
> *And keep it in a jar.*

Nobody talked for a moment.

"Does it mean anything to you, Webbers?" asked Danni.

"Sounds weird to me."

"Hm. There's only one place I've been to which fits that description of a sun. It's a bit vague, Grablet. Was there anything else?"

"That's the entire first verse."

Webbers shrugged. "Doesn't give us much to go on. What's the rest of the song?"

"Why don't we just go to the place you mentioned?" asked Danni, eager to be off. "Even if I haven't got a mould, it would be a good idea to go — just in case!"

"I agree," said the Grablet. "I'm ready!"

"You want to come too?"

"I feel like a spot of travelling," it replied. "You can't say I'll take up too much room, for I'm a portable little thing. Besides . . ." its voice took on a very crafty tone, "you need me for the rest of the song. I can't quite remember the second verse just yet."

Danni winked at Webbers. "Of course we can take the Grablet with us. It'll fit into my shirt pocket. How lucky we are to have such *important*, such *clever* company."

The Grablet purred as she popped it in her pocket and did up the zip.

As soon as Webbers had combed his hair and checked that all his pockets were properly fastened, he and Danni swallowed another yellow Mos tablet. Danni didn't even bother to glance back as they swept away from the Grablet's planet. She was much too excited about setting off for "a strange and distant star".

4

AN UNEXPECTED DIP

With the Grablet for company, the journey didn't seem very long. Snug in Danni's pocket, the Grablet sang the first verse of the Cure Song (as Danni had named it) a number of times, but still insisted it couldn't quite remember the second verse.

Then the Grablet generously asked Danni to sing one of her own songs and she happily obliged. After that, Danni described how she broke the stinking egg and her encounter with the Moldy Flizzard.

"I can't actually smell you," said the Grablet. "Perhaps you didn't get a mould after all."

Danni thought about it. She certainly didn't wish to be covered in mould but it was because she *might* be that she was having such an exciting time. Webbers interrupted her thoughts. "You'd better take this red Mos tablet, Danni. We're nearly there. See that coloured sun ahead?"

"Is that a sun? It's striped like a beachball! It's not a bit like my sun back on Earth."

"Wish I could see it," grumbled the Grablet.

"I'll tell you what it looks like," said Danni. "It's round and it's turning slowly. It's striped with every colour you can think of. There's red, yellow, green, blue, purple, pink, orange, reddish-brown, another kind of blue, a lemony colour, flamingo . . ."

"Where a sun outstrips the rainbow!" the Grablet carolled. "Sounds as if we've come to the right place."

They descended through streaky clouds to a land splashed with swathes of colour from the striped sun. Webbers was making for a blue patch and as it rose up to meet them, Danni felt her scalp tingle. Her face turned yellow and perspiration prickled the back of her neck. She couldn't seem to breathe. Her ears rang and rang with the sound of an endless schoolbell. "Webbers . . . Webbers . . ." Danni thought she was shouting but, in fact, only the faintest whisper came from her lips.

"Did you say something?" asked the Grablet.

"Sick . . . dizzy . . ." Everything went black as space.

Danni's brown eyes opened to the coloured sun, far above. It was still sending down a cornflower blue ray. She felt comfortable lying on her back, but Webbers was bending over her, looking worried.

Danni smiled drowsily. "What happened? I remember feeling dizzy and my ears were ringing. It made me feel sick. After that — nothing!"

"You fainted. I'm sorry, but one red Mos wasn't enough. I managed to push another one down your throat just then. How do you feel?"

"My head's aching. I'm okay, but I wouldn't like it to happen again."

"Nor would I!" Webbers yawned and stretched. "I had to get down in a hurry. Thought I'd never unwind the loops from your wrists because I couldn't see what I was doing. Anyway, that's all over now." He yawned again. "I have to rest before we look for the purple water. You can chat with the Grablet while I sleep." He patted a couple of pockets and opened one. From it, he took a little toy which he placed next to Danni. "Perhaps this will keep you both amused. It answers simple commands."

"He's lovely!" Danni laughed and took the Grablet from her pocket.

"About time you remembered me," it growled.

"Look at this! Look at the toy Webbers."

The toy was the image of Webbers, with the same long hair, black tube and webs, but was only about ten centimetres high.

"Pah! It's only a doll."

"So what?" said Danni. "What commands will I give him, Webbers?"

When Webbers didn't reply, Danni looked up and saw him leaning backwards at an impossible angle. Further and further back he leant, until his webs left the ground and silently floated upward. His body lay quite straight a metre from the ground, supported by absolutely nothing. His long hair streamed down like a curtain of sunshine, tinged with the sun's blue ray.

Danni forgot her headache. She sprang to her feet and gazed wonderingly at Webbers. Eyes tightly closed, a small smile curving his lips, arms neatly crossed over his chest, he was fast asleep.

"But you're up in the air," Danni whispered, and lightly touched his upper arm. Webbers' body rocked from side to side. The points on his webs shot up and circled like radar scanners. He opened his eyes and frowned.

"S . . . sorry," mumbled Danni.

"Slee . . . eee . . . eeep," sighed Webbers, closing his eyes again.

The Grablet cackled. "He's tired after all that travelling. He always sleeps like that. If anything touches him, his webs warn of danger and he wakes up."

Danni sat cross-legged near the sleeping Webbers. "It's a clever way to sleep, really. Insects can't crawl into your ears and snakes can't bite you if you're up in the air. Webbers is clever in many ways."

"He's reasonably clever," said the Grablet airily. "I notice you call him Webbers — I thought his name was some long, unpronounceable thing."

"It is, that's why I call him Webbers." Danni picked up the toy. "Shall we play with Webbers the Second?"

"Kid's stuff."

"I think he's sweet."

"It can't sing or recite poems like me. It can't talk like me. It hasn't got great intelligence like me," boasted the Grablet.

"You think a lot of yourself," retorted Danni, turning all her attention to the toy. "Now, I'm going to ask you to do something, Webbers the Second. *Walk!*"

Obediently, the toy walked forward.

"Big deal!" snorted the Grablet.

"Can *you* walk?" asked Danni.

"If I wished," replied the Grablet, "but it so happens, I don't!"

"Faster!" commanded Danni, and the webs on the toy pumped up and down, making the golden hair spread out like a fan.

"Stop!" Danni cried. The toy halted. "Lie down!" The toy stretched out on its back, webs pointing up.

Danni ran and lay down next to it, staring at the multi-coloured sun. "Did you ever see anything like it?" she mumbled.

The rigid little toy was silent, but the Grablet murmured. "I must admit, I haven't. All in all this is a very strange place, just as the Cure Song says."

Danni stood up. "Sure is strange, Grablet. There are no trees, or flowers, or grass, like on Earth. Or even any rocks, like on your place. And this can't be ground I'm standing on. It feels springy, like rubber."

"Quite mysterious," agreed the Grablet.

"Okay, Grablet of Great Intelligence! Why is the ground made of rubber?"

"I'm trying to work it out."

"While you're thinking, I'll get Webbers the Second to

do something else. Stand up, my fine little man," barked Danni, "and *march!*"

The toy stood and, arms swinging, marched stiffly as a soldier on parade. Danni giggled. "Left! Right! Left! Right! Left! Right!"

The toy went on marching, head up, shoulders back, arms swinging.

"Left! Right! Left! Right! Left! Right!"

Then it disappeared.

It took a second for Danni to understand. She stopped giggling and ran after the toy. "Where did you go to, Webbers the Second? Come back!"

"Just a moment," said the Grablet. "Slow down, Danni. I thought I heard . . ."

But Danni kept running. The toy had vanished in front of her eyes. "Come back, Webbers the Second. Where are you?" She soon found out. Her flying feet left the firm surface and for a split second ran on a whole lot of nothing, then she somersaulted and bellyflopped *splosh!* into cool blue water.

"I told you . . . glugg, glugg . . . glugg . . ." choked the Grablet. "Help . . .! glugg . . . fool . . . get me out . . . glugg . . . glugg . . ."

Up Danni bobbed, coughing and spitting. There was a nasty pain in her nose where water had gushed up her nostrils. She floated on her back, the Grablet on her chest. The Grablet gave a few exaggerated coughs and groans. "Silly, silly girl . . . cough, choke . . . you could have lost me . . . choke, cough. I *hate* water, cough, cough, choke."

"I didn't know it was there. You don't think I fell in on purpose, do you? Who could tell it was water? It's exactly the same colour as whatever it is I was standing on. Webbers the Second must have fallen in too."

"Obviously. I wanted to tell you I heard a faint splash but you wouldn't listen, would you?" complained the

27

Grablet. "Now, get me back on dry land, or dry rubber, or whatever it is. At once!"

"I have to look for the toy first. Webbers will be cross if I lose him. He must be somewhere in the water." She picked the Grablet off her chest and zipped it into her sodden pocket. Taking a deep breath, she rolled over and dived beneath the blue water. It was quite clear and she could see reasonably well, but there was no sign of Webbers the Second. Danni came up for breath, heard the Grablet hawking and spluttering and immediately dived again.

Again and again she dived, but the toy was not to be seen.

She thought she must be getting used to the water, for it didn't feel cool any more, but pleasantly warm. Then she noticed the colour changing. The water was no longer a bright, cornflower blue but a faded yellow-blue. Looking at the sun, Danni understood what was happening. The sun had kept revolving, the blue period was ending and the next coloured stripe to shine down on her was orange.

"See that, Grablet?"

"SEE??? *I can't see anything! I am imprisoned in a soggy pocket and have nearly been drowned countless times!!!*"

"Sorry," said Danni. "The blue stripe is ending and we're going into an orange stripe. The water's getting warmer and I'm getting out."

"About time too!"

"I've looked everywhere for the little toy, but I can't find him. Hope Webbers isn't too mad at me."

"Don't ever take me for a swim again!"

Danni swam to the rubber ledge from which she had tumbled into the water. It was higher than she'd thought. Reaching up, she grabbed the edge and heaved the top half of her body out of the water. She was almost balancing on the ledge when her hands slipped. *Plop!* Back she splashed into the water. She tried again and the same thing happened.

"Get me out of here!" yelled the Grablet.

The water was no longer warm. It was hot. And it was a definite orange colour. Danni tried to get out by hooking one foot and one hand over the ledge and hauling herself out like a crab. It didn't work. The rubber was warm and slippery and she lost her grip, plopping back into the water again.

"What are you *doing*?" moaned the Grablet. "Get me out, I said!"

"I'm trying!"

"Try again!"

"It's getting much too hot," Danni sobbed. "I have to get out, I can hardly breathe." The water was a steaming sauna, the ledge as slippery as a seal. "It's no good, Grablet . . . I can't get out and I've gone all weak and tired."

"Call for Webbers," cried the Grablet. "I don't want to be cooked!"

"HELP! *Webbers, can you hear me? We're being boiled! Webbers, wake up!*"

The Grablet joined in. "*Wake up, Webbers. Save me! SAVE ME!*"

But Webbers didn't answer.

"He's still asleep," gasped Danni. "What'll we do now? . . . AAAHHH!"

"What is it? What happened?" shrieked the Grablet.

Danni screamed again as something brushed against her a second time. A bronze shape rose beneath her thrashing legs and, suddenly, she was straddling something. Swifter than a jet-ski, she was carried out of the steaming orange water and into refreshingly cool blue water. She passed through that and went skimming through warmish, coral-coloured water; then tingling yellow, followed by humid brown, crisp green and moderate fawn to a cosy terracotta shade.

"What's happening? Have you forgotten me? How I hate being in this pocket," groaned the Grablet. "Danni! Danni!

Where are we? What happened?"

"Wheee!" Danni whooped. "A funny thing happened. I think I'm riding a fish. A big fish. It's carried me through different colours and, you know, Grablet, each colour feels different. Some are hot, some are cold and some are in between."

"A *fish*!" shrieked the Grablet. "It might want to eat us!"

"I don't think so. It would have eaten us by now if it was hungry. I think it's rescuing us. Don't be ungrateful, Grablet."

As Danni said this, she felt the fish hump its back and for a wild second thought the Grablet might be right. Instead, she was smartly tossed up and out of the water. She landed with a bounce on firm rubber the same colour as the terracotta water.

Scrambling to her feet, she was just in time to see a shape like a bronze sweet potato disappearing underwater. "Thanks a lot,"she called. "Thanks for saving me and the Grablet."

"Can I come out of this pocket now?" pleaded the Grablet.

"We both had a hot bath," said Danni, as she took it out. "All the mud from my duckpen has been washed off. See, I'm clean as a whistle."

"That's all right for you, but I didn't need a bath. I *never* need baths," grumbled the Grablet. It made a yawning sound and bubbles came out of its holes. "I'm fair tuckered out. Can you blow the water out of me please?"

Danni blew through the holes until it looked as if the Grablet was quite dry. She put it down while she took off her wet shirt and sandals. "My clothes should dry soon," she said. "This colour is warm and friendly, don't you think? Like garden pots."

The Grablet snored. In the cosy light, it looked as if it was made of the softest leather.

Danni smiled and stroked the Grablet. "Webbers is sure

Danni gave the Grablet a shake to wake it.

"*Erk!*" was the first thing the Grablet said. "What's that awful smell?"

"It must be me. There's a mould growing on my toe."

"*Gurk!* Pity I have such a good sense of smell. You really pong!"

"I can't help it. Can you remember the next verse of the Cure Song? It's urgent now. I don't want to turn into a mouldy egg."

"Nor do I! Make sure you don't touch *me* with that toe."

"It's best to cover your whole foot," said Webbers. He went through his pockets, turning out a pack of cards, two crumpled envelopes, a pair of spectacles, something that looked like netting, two jars of green powder, a safety pin, a bookmark and a packet of dried bananas before coming up with one red-and-black striped woollen sock. "Here, put this on. It'll hold back the smell."

The sock was too big. Danni rolled the top over a few times. "Haven't you got another? One sock looks pretty silly."

"I don't usually carry socks," said Webbers vaguely. "Can't remember where I got that one."

"Well, I don't suppose it matters who sees me like this," sighed Danni. "We'd better get the purple water now. Can we use one of those jars? What's that green stuff?"

"Can't remember. Those jars have been in my pockets for ages. Anyway, the purple water is more important." Webbers upended one of the jars and the green powder formed a little pyramid by his webs. "Now we have a jar, let's get the water, Danni." He started cramming everything back into his pockets.

Danni hastily grabbed the dried bananas. "Are these for some NITT experiment, Webbers, or can I have them? I'm starving!"

"Of course you can have them. They're nothing to do with NITT." Webbers scratched his ear. "I must have picked

33

them up somewhere."

Danni prodded the Grablet as she chewed the leathery, wrinkled brown strips. "Hurry up and remember the second verse please."

"It's coming, girl. It's coming."

"There's a purple area a few stripes away," said Webbers, turning his back for Danni to hold on to the loops.

The purple area was neither warm nor cool. Danni felt as if someone had placed a light, velvet cloak over her. Webbers rinsed out the jar and half-filled it with purple water. "How much is a dash, I wonder?"

"Less than that," said Danni. "Mum uses a dash of this and that in her cooking and it's usually just a few drops."

Webbers poured out most of the water and held up the jar for Danni to inspect. The water glistened amethyst. "The first step towards your cure, Danni."

"The second step is the second verse," said Danni. "What is it, Grablet?"

The Grablet didn't hesitate. It sang:

> Where a plant is food for all,
> And a shadow haunts each quarter,
> Take a fresh and tender leaf,
> And soak it in the water.

Danni whooped. "Good on you, Grablet!" Then she frowned. " 'A shadow haunts each quarter.' That doesn't sound good. The Moldy Flizzard has a huge shadow."

"I know a place where a plant is food for all," said Webbers. "In fact, I have a very good friend there whom I've been promising to visit for a long time."

"What's the place called?"

"Bearakha. My friend is Boris of Bearakha."

"Then it's not Zubel, where the Flizzards come from?"

Webbers laughed and took out his mirror. "No Danni.

Well, are we all well rested and ready to go? It's a long, long way to Bearakha."

"It's nice for you to have a friend there," said Danni. "Nobody seems to live here on these rubber things."

"Mattresses," said Webbers, smoothing his hair.

"What?"

"These things are rubber mattresses."

"So they are! You didn't know that did you, Grablet?"

"I was just about to tell you," lied the Grablet.

"I wonder how the mattresses got here," said Danni.

"The Universe is full of mysteries," replied the Grablet.

"Is that another way of saying you don't know?"

"Right." The Grablet cackled. "I don't have a clue."

After Webbers had put the jar of purple water safely away with his mirror, both he and Danni swallowed a Mos tablet. Danni took hold of the shoulder loops. Just before her feet left the rubber mattress, she called out: "Goodbye, and thank you, whoever you are."

There was a flurry in the purple water and a swollen sweet potato shape with trailing whiskers appeared. A gleaming thing, which could have been an eye, winked at Danni then disappeared in another flurry, leaving the water calm and unruffled again.

As they flew up through the streaky clouds, Danni said, "Imagine Webbers the Second still marching underwater. I'm sorry I didn't have time to play with him longer. At least he'll be company for that nice whiskery thing that saved me."

"If you'd only known about the water, you could have asked the toy to swim," said Webbers.

Webbers had not been exaggerating when he said it was a long way to Bearakha. Danni was able to sing a number of her songs to the Grablet, to listen to some spirited poems, and to have a long and refreshing nap before a very bright planet beckoned through the blackness of space.

"Is that Bearakha?" she asked. "Don't forget to give me

a strong Mos tablet this time, will you?"

"You won't need one here," replied Webbers. "According to Boris, the atmosphere is about the same as the one you're used to on Earth." Soon his breathing changed to short gasps and they began descending. It was dark and Danni found she was breathing quite easily. They landed among some plants, which swayed to and fro in a fresh breeze.

Danni dropped the loops and asked eagerly, "Will you be seeing Boris now?" When Webbers didn't reply, she peered through the darkness and saw his pale webs floating upward. She remembered then that Webbers must be very tired after such a long journey and would need plenty of sleep. Unfortunately, she wasn't the least bit tired herself. After a while, she whispered to her pocket: "Are you awake, Grablet?"

"Mmm?" croaked a sleepy voice.

"We've landed on Bearakha and Webbers is sleeping. It's dark and I'm lonely."

A yawn came from the pocket. "Very well. Take me out if you must." When the Grablet was perched on Danni's palm, it immediately launched into a rambling description of "a perfectly lovely dream". It lasted so long the darkness changed to early-morning light and Danni saw they had landed in a field of trumpet-shaped, lilac flowers, stretching in every direction as far as she could see.

"So that was that," said the Grablet, finishing at last.

Danni stretched. "I wonder if these flowers ever end? Look, there's a hill over there. We should get a good view from the top."

"Lead on," said the Grablet. "This breeze makes a strange noise, don't you think?"

Danni listened, but couldn't hear anything unusual. Holding the Grablet and humming, she set off for the hill. She didn't get far. After about twenty steps, her foot caught in a writhing root and she crashed to the ground.

"Whoops!" cried the Grablet, as a tent of green leaves

closed over them. "Be careful of me!"

Danni was about to snap a reply when a weird screeching noise took her mind right off the Grablet. The noise made hairs rise at the back of her neck. It set her teeth on edge and gave her goose pimples. It made her think of an evil organ played in a dark castle by a dribbling monster. It was a noise of zombies rising from the grave, of vampires wakening from their coffins, of werewolves howling in the woods at night.

The terrible noise hypnotised Danni and the Grablet. Both stayed silent in their leafy tent. From head to heel, Danni trembled. She couldn't stop. The noise was now directly above. Through the broad leaves, she glimpsed a shadow, dark as a rain cloud. "What's that?" she whispered.

"Something horrible," replied the Grablet hoarsely. "Please don't let it get me!"

The shadow passed, but Danni stayed hidden in the leaves.

"We can't stay here all day," whispered the Grablet. "Is Webbers all right?"

Although she didn't want to, Danni cautiously sat up. She looked over her shoulder. To her horror, she saw a leaden, swirling mist gathered directly over the sleeping body of Webbers. She saw his web points circling, but it was too late. Tendrils of the mist wrapped about him. The hideous screeching noise grew twice as loud. Even as Danni started to her feet and ran, shouting, back the way she had come, the black-hearted mist gathered up Webbers and moved rapidly away across the flower fields.

"Put him down! Leave Webbers alone!" cried Danni.

But the mist disappeared into the distance, taking with it the last strains of hellish music.

Danni's shoulders sagged. "Webbers is gone . . ." she said, disbelievingly. "What'll I do, Grablet? Will I follow that mist thing?"

"That must be the shadow which 'haunts each quarter'," quavered the Grablet. "Whatever it is, it moves much too fast for you to catch up. And what would you do if you did? I think we should find Boris first."

"You're right," Danni agreed. "He'll help us look for Webbers." Not knowing which direction to take, she started for the hill again, this time picking her steps more carefully.

"Stop!" commanded the Grablet. "I hear something."

Obediently, Danni halted. Was that dreadful mist returning for her? Faintly, she heard: "Halloo! Halloo!"

"Someone's coming," she said.

"Certainly, but is it a friendly someone?"

Three men topped the crest of the hill.

"It's not an 'it'. It's three 'he's'," cried Danni, waving both arms. "We have to take the chance that they're friendly."

The men hurried down the hill. When they drew closer, Danni saw they looked just like each other. They had long faces, long noses, hounds' ears and tiny eyes. Each wore a very short tunic of stringy fibre. Unsmiling, they stood in front of her.

"Please help," she begged. "It's taken Webbers."

They seemed to know exactly what she meant, for, together, they said: "The Skreek!"

"If the Skreek is something that sounds frightful and looks like a dark mist then that's what took Webbers, all right," said the Grablet.

The men stared at the Grablet, perched on Danni's hand.

"We heard you shouting," said one, "and we knew the Skreek had struck again."

"We must go after it," said Danni.

"Immediately," added the Grablet.

The man shook his head. "Nobody can follow the Skreek."

Danni snorted. "Well *I'm* going to follow it!"

"Me too," piped up the Grablet.

The three men stared at the Grablet so long that Danni stamped her foot impatiently. "If you won't help us, then can you take me to Boris of Bearakha please?"

"He'll be back at The Poles," muttered one of the men, and he hoisted Danni onto his shoulders. They set off, striding over the carpet of lilac flowers. The landscape was quite flat apart from two hills, and they seemed to travel very quickly. The men spoke little and did not smile, but Danni didn't care. She was much too anxious about Webbers to start up any conversation.

Eventually they came to a place where short, thick poles were stuck in the ground. Each pole had a ring on top and through each ring was a slender rope attached to a huge balloon. The lilac flowers grew up to and around the poles. At the fifth pole, the men stopped. The man carrying Danni cupped his hands and called upwards to the gently swaying balloon. "Ho! Boris! Boris!"

One half of a trapdoor was flung open at the bottom of the balloon. A man's head appeared. He looked exactly like the other three men.

"Gardeners from the West Field," explained the man carrying Danni. He lifted her from his shoulders. "We found this stranger wandering in the field. Apparently the Skreek took her friend."

The man in the balloon opened the other half of the trapdoor and lowered himself to the ground by a flexible metal ladder. He stood in front of Danni, tall and strong, the only features marking him from the others being his extra height and a thick, leather bracelet on his left wrist. The bracelet was studded with ruby-coloured stones. Tucked behind it was a knife.

6

STOWAWAY DANNI

"Hello, Boris," said Danni, looking up at his blank, fixed face. "I came here with Webbers."

"Psst!" hissed the Grablet. "Give his right name, you idiot!"

"I mean Kroning . . . Kronig . . . something," gabbled Danni. "Anyway, he comes from Lex and has long golden hair and webs."

Boris's small eyes flashed. "Kroninkliwzotl?"

"Yes, that's him! We came here to get something very important, and also to see you. After we landed, Webbers was sleeping and that Skreek carried him off. A terrible, awful noise came from it!"

Boris's long cheeks were stretched taut as a drumskin. He smashed his fists together. "After such a long time, my good friend comes to see me and that *thing* has to . . .!" He paused, glared at the three men and said, "We have to find him!"

Danni shouted. The Grablet crowed. But the three gardeners shook their heads. Boris frowned at them. "I know it seems hopeless," he said, "but the Skreek has taken a dear companion of the past. I'll do anything to find him." With that, he put three fingers in his mouth and whistled. From the surrounding balloons, men hurried down metal ladders. They hastened to Boris and grouped themselves neatly in front of him.

"We'll see some action now," the Grablet murmured. "He seems to be a boss of some sort."

Wasting no words, Boris began. "This stranger arrived on Bearakha with a friend of mine. The Skreek has carried off my friend. I intend to do everything possible to save him," his nostrils twitched, "even if it means crossing The Waste."

The men's tiny eyes widened to the size of dried peas.

"Who will come with me?" asked Boris. "I need six."

Not one spoke. Danni broke the deathly silence. "Please!" she cried. "We must start right now!"

To her dismay, Boris shook his head. "I'm sorry, but *you* definitely cannot come. We must travel extremely dangerous and unknown paths."

"But I must . . ." began Danni.

"We have to!" protested the Grablet.

"I won't hear of it!" barked Boris, ignoring them. He looked at his men. "Well?"

Reluctantly, the three gardeners from the West Field stepped forward. A second later, two men from the back shouldered their way to the front. Danni whispered: "If another man doesn't come forward, he'll have to take me instead." But the last man did step forward and Danni wept with disappointment.

Informing the whole group that he and the six men would be leaving immediately, Boris ordered food and water to be brought. He gave another whistle, lower in pitch than the first, and a woman came down the ladder from his balloon. Her features were very like those of the men.

Boris turned to face Danni again. "This is my wife, Beta."

"I am called Danni," mumbled Danni. "And this is the Grablet."

Beta nodded and looked suspiciously at the Grablet. "How do?" said the Grablet, but she didn't reply.

"During my absence," Boris told his wife, "you are to care for Danni and . . . er . . . her friend. If I do not return within one month, you must take her to Old Wen who will unlock my sealed cube for instructions on how to return her to her own place." With that, he glanced once at Danni and strode away.

"A month?" Danni's legs threatened to give way, and she grabbed at Beta. "A month? He doesn't know . . . he doesn't realise . . . I can't wait a month!" Her clutching fingers left white marks on Beta's bare arm. "If I don't find Webbers and get on with collecting things for the Cure, I'll be covered in mould. It won't be worth sending me back to Earth after a month. By then I'll be a giant, smelly, walking fungus!"

But Beta couldn't understand. She tapped her head as if Danni was crazy. "Go up the ladder to the balloon," she ordered.

People were scurrying around The Poles. Large containers and bundles were being loaded into odd vehicles which looked like teacups without handles. The cups were open to the air and had simple instrument panels with forward and reverse levers and handles for going upwards and downwards.

"Please, Beta, can I watch them leave?" asked Danni, trying desperately to think of a way to escape and join the search party.

Beta looked at her blankly. She shrugged. "I suppose so," she said at last, "but stay next to me."

They stood at the bottom of the ladder, watching the hasty preparations. Two men sat in each of three vehicles. Boris sat alone in a fourth cup giving last-minute instructions. On a signal from him, the handle in each cup was given a smart jerk. The cups moved smoothly upward.

Wah-boom! A double explosion thundered from one

of the cups. The cup billowed a trail of greasy smoke. Sparks sizzled and crackled and it dropped like a shooting star, landing with a *whump* in the midst of the lilac flowers with the two men inside slumped to one side.

There were gasps and cries and everyone hurried to help, including Danni and Beta. The men were pulled clear of the smoking cup and Danni watched an old man with fine white hair tending them. A sigh went up from the anxious crowd as the old man pronounced the men stunned, but alive.

Meanwhile, the other cups had landed. Boris stood near the two unlucky men, rubbing his forehead. "Not a good omen," he muttered.

Danni had seen her chance. As Beta and the rest of the crowd watched the unconscious men being carried away, Danni sneaked unnoticed to Boris's cup. Heart thumping, she clambered in, slithered under the bundles and lay still as a snake on the floor.

The cup lurched as Boris climbed in. His voice sounded muffled as he gave the command signal. The cup rose upward, paused four metres above ground and moved forward. Danni had made it. It was very uncomfortable lying cramped beneath prickly bundles, but Danni wanted to stay there as long as she could stand it, for fear of Boris turning back to The Poles if he discovered her too soon.

After a while, the Grablet must have slept, for Danni heard faint snores. A leaf popped out of a bundle and tickled her nose.

"*Ah choo!*"

"*Yah!*" yelled the Grablet.

"Come out of there! Who's that?" demanded Boris.

Shaking off bundles and containers, Danni crawled to the front of the cup and edged onto the seat next to Boris. Too nervous to look at him, she stared at the Grablet, clasped in her fist. Danni waited and waited for Boris to say something, but he kept his thin lips firmly closed. When she couldn't wait any longer, she mumbled, "We had to come, Boris. Webbers is our friend too, and we're very worried about him. Apart from that, I need him more than you can imagine."

"We're not afraid of danger — in fact we like it," said the Grablet unconvincingly.

Boris frowned. "It's too late to take you back. We've lost too much time already." When Danni looked up and smiled, he added: "But don't think I'm happy about it!"

Danni tried to think of something to please him. She remembered an ancient packet of chewing gum she'd had in her shirt pocket. It was still there, looking very battered, but Boris shook his head when she presented it to him. The Grablet offered to recite an epic poem of derring-do. Boris curtly refused and the Grablet was very hurt.

Thinking it best to annoy Boris as little as possible, Danni sat back and chewed the gum herself. On and on they journeyed, over endless fields of flowers. Towards dusk, Danni saw the fields thinning out. First, fingers of sand crept into the flowers, and then there were no flowers at all, just desert and a few stones.

"The Waste," explained Boris.

It seemed much warmer, even sticky. A heavy weight appeared to hang over them. The three cups were flying close together, with Boris in the lead. Occasionally, Danni turned to check on the other cups. Once when she was doing this, she noticed something strange. "There's a brown thing following us!" she exclaimed. "It's not the Skreek, thank goodness!"

"What? What brown thing?" piped the Grablet. "Where?"

"Behind us," said Danni. "It's skinny and . . . and . . . it's not really flying. I mean, not like Webbers does. It seems to sort of *wriggle* through the air!"

Boris didn't seemed surprised. "She had to come," he muttered. "It's the Watcher of The Waste. She won't do anything yet. It's getting dark and she hasn't got night eyes."

"What?" asked Danni.

"Who?" asked the Grablet.

"The Watcher of The Waste," repeated Boris. "She can't see at night." And despite further questions, that was all he would say. They flew on, into darkness. It was so dark Danni could no longer see the brown wriggler, but she could still just make out the cups following them.

Steadily chewing, she pinched herself to stay awake. "Where are we going?" she asked. "And how do you know that Webbers will be there?"

"The Skreek always goes in the same direction. Towards the Dreaded Towers. It takes all its victims there. We don't know why, because since the Watcher began patrolling The Waste no-one has ever returned from a journey through it."

Danni shuddered. "Poor Webbers!" She imagined all sorts of terrible things happening to her friend.

Boris's hard face softened just a fraction. "Webbers, as you call him, is not easily defeated. I'll do everything I can to save him, Danni."

"Webbers is quite smart," comforted the Grablet. "Not as clever as me, of course, but I'm sure he can hold out until we ride to the rescue."

Danni made another check on the cups behind them. Nothing glimmered through the darkness. "I can't see the others!" she cried.

"What! We must not become separated!" Boris turned to look for himself. As he did so, Danni's insides were nearly jolted outside. Her feet shot up to meet her ears and she was deafened by a mighty crash. The Grablet torpedoed out of her hand and their cup shattered into a thousand pieces. Boris and Danni catapulted forward. A split second later, they plummeted down, down through the air.

This is the end of me, thought Danni. I'll be spread all over the desert. Instead, she back-flipped onto something very soft. Hardly daring to believe it, she stood up and gingerly wiggled her limbs, one by one. Nothing wrong. Only the chewing gum had been dislodged — it was now wedged on the end of her nose. Danni soon got rid of that.

Jet-black was the night. Nervously, she tried a few steps, touching scattered bundles and containers. "Boris," she whispered, "are you there? Grablet, where are you?"

Danni's answer was a strong arm wrapped about her waist, a thick hand over her mouth. "It's me," Boris whispered in her ear. "Make no noise at all. We're being trailed."

She didn't need to be told twice. Hand in hand with Boris, she padded away from the wreckage, her feet sinking into soft, billowing material. Every few steps, they paused and listened. Danni strained her ears for a sound from the Grablet. Her hearing had almost recovered from the noise of the crash and now she picked up heavy breathing sounds and a slight whirring noise. Danni didn't think they came from the Grablet. The sounds were irregular, excited, and somehow repulsive.

They reached the end of the soft material, stumbled, and fell onto desert sand. Danni heard a harsh grunt, followed by an exasperated curse. No . . . it definitely wasn't the Grablet! They fled. Long after they could no longer hear the breathing, they threw themselves flat on the sand.

"I lost the Grablet," gasped Danni, "when the cup hit whatever it was that we hit."

"We'll look for it tomorrow, if we get the chance," puffed Boris.

Although Danni would have liked to search for the Grablet right away, she had no wish to return and face the owner of the heavy breathing, especially at night. For the rest of the night hours, she slept fitfully while Boris stayed awake and watchful.

In the morning, the desert stretched about them, white and dry as sugar. They crawled to a higgledy pile of stones, hoping to use them as a shelter.

"The Watcher is sure to come and see if we've been destroyed," said Boris. "We must stay out of sight."

The stones made a reasonable hiding place and they crouched in a sort of cave, peering out towards the place from which they had run during the night. They saw a towering stone wall with a long fat contraption, like a pale sausage, at the foot.

"No wonder we crashed!" said Danni, looking at the solid wall and the wreckage of their cup strewn willy-nilly on the billowy material.

Boris squeezed her hand. "Quiet!"

A little man, fat as a cushion, was running up and down the pale sausage. He was dressed in a bottle-green jumper and wore only one boot. His feet sank into the soft sausage, and he kept picking up containers and bundles and tossing them around in a frenzy. Without warning, he gave up his frantic search and bounced on tiny feet. Quite distinctly, Danni heard his cry of rage.

"*Naaaooowww! Naaaooowww!*"

As he lifted his head for the first time, his face was revealed. It was perfectly round, with saucepan-lid eyes. He had a single ear, and that was black and curved like a button. When he opened his wailing mouth, needle-sharp teeth glittered like python's fangs.

7

THE DREADED TOWERS

Danni shuddered. "He's horrible! I think he's looking for us!"

"He must be the breather we heard last night," whispered Boris. "Now I know why others have never returned from The Waste!"

A silent shadow undulated over the desert in front of their stones. A moment later, a tightly robed figure landed next to the little man on the sausage. It was very tall, and thin as a flagpole. Any face it might have had was covered by a hood.

"The Watcher of The Waste," breathed Boris into Danni's ear.

A thread-fine feeler emerged from the Watcher's copper-coloured robe. It seized the little man by the arm. "You were supposed to let them in through the gap, you greedy worm," rasped a reedy voice. "Your job is to stop them getting out . . . NOT IN! The Minister will be very angry when he hears of this!"

"The Minister has enough slaves. Anyway, they got away from me," whined the little man. He waddled over to his missing boot, which lay near a burst container. He tugged at the boot until it came up with skinny spaghetti strands sticking to the sole. "I couldn't even chase them because my boot got stuck in this stuff," he sulked. "I nearly had them but they ran off into The Waste."

The two of them argued for a while, then the Watcher reached up and pulled an iron lever set high in the wall. A whole section of the wall folded down, leaving a doorway through which the Watcher dragged the little man. After they disappeared through the gap, the wall unfolded upward again, as if it had never been altered.

Boris and Danni could relax at last.

Danni managed a giggle. "His boot got stuck in my chewing gum."

For the first time, Danni saw Boris's lips form a small smile. "You stay here," he said. "I'll see if I can find the Grablet."

Leaving their shelter, he dashed over the sand and jumped onto the soft white sausage. The Grablet is sure to call out now that it's safe to do so, Danni told herself.

Boris made a thorough search, lifting up debris and scouring the sausage centimetre by centimetre. Danni's heart began to sink. Why wasn't the Grablet calling out? Where was it? She watched Boris gather up a container which was still intact and an armful of bundles. He hurried back to the stone shelter. "No sign of the Grablet," he said.

Danni's bottom lip quivered. "Now both Webbers *and* the Grablet have gone! So many nasty things have happened on Bearakha."

"You've been very brave so far," said Boris. "Don't give up. All is not yet lost." He took the lid off the container and poured water into it for Danni to drink. In the bundles were stems, leaves and flowers of the plant Danni had seen growing everywhere but in The Waste. Boris wolfed into some leaves.

" 'Where a plant is food for all'," quoted Danni.

"What's that?"

"Is that what you eat all the time?"

Boris nodded. "This plant has been our only source of food for many years. Why don't you try some?"

Danni nibbled at a stem. It was quite pleasant, so she ate a few flowers.

"Through there is where we must go to find Webbers and the Grablet," announced Boris, pointing at the wall.

Feeling much better after something to eat and drink, Danni stood. "Let's go now," she said. They scurried over the sand and Boris helped Danni to climb onto the sausage. By standing on two containers, Boris could just reach the lever in the wall. He gave it a tug and the wall folded down. On the other side were steps. Swallowing her fear, Danni walked down the steps followed by Boris. When they reached the bottom step, a trigger mechanism was set off and the wall unfolded upwards, closing the entrance behind them.

They looked ahead.

Some distance away, at the end of a winding road, was a gloomy looking mansion with seven towers soaring into the sky. It looked sullen and distorted, like a monstrous crowned spider which squatted, waiting for its prey.

Danni could just make out the Watcher of The Waste and the little man in the green jumper entering one of the many doorways leading into the mansion. She took Boris's hand. Heads turning this way and that, like nervous pussycats, they padded towards the Dreaded Towers.

"Seven towers," counted Danni, "and seven doorways. Is that why you wanted seven men?"

Boris grunted. "Yes. Keep your eyes on the door they went through."

"Who's this Minister they mentioned?"

"I don't know."

As they drew nearer to the Dreaded Towers, Danni's ears caught faint strains of the ghastly music she remembered coming from the Skreek. She moved closer to Boris.

Because there were so many doors to watch and because all the doors were as black as night, their eyes played tricks on them. Having reached the end of the road, and climbed three stone steps to grey slate flagging surrounding the mansion, it became impossible to tell through which door the Watcher and the little man had entered.

Both had tried to concentrate, but they couldn't agree on which one it was.

"This is it," said Danni, reaching for a scrolled handle in the shape of an S.

"No. The one next to that,' insisted Boris, reaching to her left.

"Or it could have been this," continued Danni, pointing to the door on her right.

"This is ridiculous!" snorted Boris.

"We have to start somewhere," said Danni, sounding braver than she felt. She turned the handle she had first touched. The black door was old, deeply pitted with the scars of ages, and very heavy. Danni shoved with her shoulder and it swung open, creaking on brass hinges.

"I'll go first, if you don't mind." Boris strode in front, holding Danni back and listening for a few seconds before pulling the door closed. Inside, the hum of Skreek music was much louder. Danni tried not to think about it.

Stretching ahead was a bare and shadowy corridor, lit here and there by flickering lamps. Doors led off the corridor at regular intervals.

They began on tiptoe. At some of the doors, they stopped and listened, but heard nothing other than the strange Skreek music. The corridor forked. There wasn't a soul on either fork and Boris decided to turn left. The passage started winding upward. Danni thought they must have walked for at least half an hour before they saw a wedge of light coming from a door left ajar. Gusts of steam blew through the crack into the corridor, bringing a whiff of curry.

Tiptoeing up, they peeped in.

Five men moved very swiftly around a wooden table

in a room which shone with metal sinks and benches. The men were placing things which sizzled and steamed onto ornate golden platters.

"Some sort of kitchen," whispered Boris.

"Those men are moving awfully quickly," replied Danni, puzzled. Then she noticed that the kitchen hands were all wearing roller skates! "How peculiar," she whispered, nudging Boris to see for himself.

Boris led her away from the door. "If this is the kitchen," he said, "they might be preparing dinner for whoever is in charge. The Minister, perhaps. I think we should follow and see where this food is served."

Almost as if this was a signal, the men glided out of the kitchen on their roller skates. Before them, they pushed a silver trolley piled with golden platters, engulfed in clouds of steam. Danni and Boris pressed into the shadows between two lamps and the strange procession swept by without noticing them.

The men and their trolley zoomed off down the corridor. First they travelled back the way Boris and Danni had come and then they went straight ahead along the right fork. The two companions raced to keep up, but the trolley drew further and further ahead. Soon they lost sight of it as it whisked around a bend in the corridor. They had to trust their ears and follow the rumble of distant wheels.

Panting and perspiring, they came at last to a heavily brocaded curtain which had been drawn partly aside by a tasselled rope. Boris slipped behind it. Danni crouched under his arm. Pressing their cheeks to the wall, they spied into a cavernous hall.

In the centre of the hall was an oval table of inkiest ebony. Three figures sat at the table. Danni recognised two.

One was the tall and skinny Watcher of The Waste. On her breast, a yellow diamond stickpin, in the shape of a dagger, flashed in the light from a hundred candles. She sat ramrod stiff, one feeler clutching a filigreed goblet.

The other figure Danni recognised was the little man in the bottle-green jumper. He looked very frightened. His black ear was spinning like a top and a glistening river of sweat flowed from his forehead to his snub nose, where it formed into droplets and drip, dripped onto his wringing hands. Every now and then, he sniffed repulsively.

The third figure was quite an ordinary looking man wearing a flowing gown of deepest plum. He had thick, purplish lips and six oily strands of hair combed straight as railway tracks on the top of his head. This man was being served with one of the steaming golden platters from the silver trolley.

Danni narrowed her spying eye to see what was on the platter — it was just one curried shrimp.

The man in plum picked up a golden knife and fork and delicately sliced the hot shrimp into six pieces. Then he gathered the pieces together and rubbed them into his head. One of the roller skaters immediately laid a second golden platter, containing another steaming shrimp, before him. This time, the man ate the shrimp. As soon as he had finished, he received another, and he ate that one too.

He likes very fast service, thought Danni, watching the waiters scooting around the trolley. Their skates were of brass and the straps went right up to their ankles and right down to their . . . Danni blinked. The roller skaters had no toes! No toes at all!

All of Danni's toes, including the mouldy one, began to tingle with alarm.

The little man was offered no food. As the waiters whizzed around their trolley, Danni noticed him greedily flick his lips with a pointed tongue. The Watcher of The Waste also sat without food, but occasionally she sipped from the filigreed goblet.

The man in plum continued eating until he had consumed five curried shrimps, after which he leaned back in his carved chair and waved the skaters away.

The roller skaters cleared the table, leaving only the candles, and departed so rapidly that Danni was flicked in the eye by the flapping curtain. She peered into the hall again. The man in plum was picking his teeth with a golden toothpick. He sighed contentedly, leaning back, rubbing his paunch and gazing happily at the many statues of himself which lined the walls of the great hall.

Abruptly, his manner changed. He stiffened. He glowered at the Watcher. "Where are my new ones? You said they would be here last night."

"Minister, all preparations were made as soon as the cups entered The Waste," droned the evil voice of the Watcher, "but I had to go back and follow them after I reported to you. Unfortunately, it was late, night was coming and . . ." her voice took on a whingeing note, "as you know, I lost the gift of night sight some time ago."

The Minister nodded impatiently.

"Two of the cups must have veered off in the wrong direction, for I have not traced them since nightfall. The third cup was to have flown through the break in the wall but . . ." the Watcher's hooded head swivelled towards the little man and she said maliciously, "Skive, here, thought he'd try some tricks of his own!"

Skive tried to shrink.

"I don't know how, but he closed the gap and let the cup crash in the hope of something for himself. Somehow, the man and child travelling in the cup managed to escape," concluded the Watcher.

The Minister's face bloomed as scarlet as Danni's shirt. "You treacherous glutton!" he shouted at Skive. "Don't I treat you well? Don't you have enough fun with the silly fools who try to escape?"

Skive sweated even more freely.

"How did a runt like you close the gap and manage to

get back on the other side of the wall, anyway?" demanded the Minister.

"I can jump on the steps and bounce right over the wall," gabbled Skive quite proudly. "I can also bounce up to reach the lever. Do you want me to show you how I can bounce?" He rolled off his chair.

"*No!*" roared the Minister. "I've a good mind to give you to the Skreek. At least I have one faithful servant who brings me slaves instead of trying to take them from me." He leered at Skive. "I've never given the faithful Skreek a present. Nobody knows just what the Skreek desires the most. Would you like to be the first to find out?"

Skive's look of pride vanished and his terror returned. His saucepan-lid eyes roved the hall as if seeking escape. His upper lip drew back from his fangs for an instant. Then he reluctantly reached under his jumper and brought out a dented tin.

"What's this?" hissed the Watcher.

Slowly, Skive unscrewed the top. He sniffed. He drew out an object which he tenderly laid on the ebony table. "I've brought you a special gift, my Minister," he crooned in a silky voice.

The object immediately gave a piercing shriek which made both the Minister and the Watcher jump half a metre out of their chairs.

The Minister recovered his dignity and frowned. "What is it?" he asked. With shaky hand, he reached over and gingerly picked up the Grablet.

"*Put me down at once!*"

The Minister dropped the Grablet like a hot scone.

"It came from the cup which crashed. It hit me on the head," explained Skive, eyeing the Grablet covetously.

"*Help! I've been stolen!*" yelled the Grablet.

"Ssh! Not so loud!" demanded the Minister, holding his ears.

"What is this piece of nonsense?" rasped the Watcher jealously.

"Shut up! Let me go! Help! Help!"

"Will you be quiet!" ordered the Minister. He picked up the Grablet and shook it like a salt shaker.

The Grablet disobeyed. "NO, *I won't! How dare you talk to me like that, Prune-lip!"*

The Minister ground his teeth. "I'm not sure I care for this gift."

"I'll have it back if you don't want it," slobbered Skive, eagerly holding out his hand.

"None of your insolence!" thundered the Minister.

"Help! The Grablet's been stolen by a bunch of kooks!" shrieked the Grablet.

"I'll take no more of this!" spluttered the Minister. "I'll put you away until you learn more respect." Rising, he dropped the Grablet into the middle drawer of a small, ivory cabinet and closed the drawer with a bang. The Grablet was cut off in mid-shriek.

The Minister smiled nastily. "I'll see to that problem later."

Danni saw Skive scowl. His cold eyes flicked towards the drawer.

"As I was saying, Skive, I should give you to the Skreek. However . . ." The Minister reflected for a few moments. "You're lucky I need you and your ear. No-one else can detect the throb of a heartbeat like you can."

Danni's heart skipped.

The Minister continued. "I need both of you to help find these wanderers in The Waste. There can be no permanent escape for them. You will search by land, particularly at night, Skive. And you," he turned to the Watcher, "will search by day." Louder, he added, "Keep moving at all times!"

"But I hate walking," moaned Skive, sniffing disgustingly. "Besides, I've got a bad cold and it's given me earache and I don't know if I'll be able to hear prop . . ."

"Silence!" roared the Minister. "Both of you are to leave immediately. And remember, if you fail, the Skreek will welcome you both!" He pounded his fist on the table. "They can't be far away. Go and find them!"

8

HELP FROM A ROLLER SKATER

Echoing the Minister's voice, the infernal music of the Skreek rose for a moment in the background before sinking back to a regular hum.

The Watcher of The Waste and Skive bowed low to the Minister. Danni cowered behind the brocade curtain. What if Skive could hear her heart beating? It sounded as loud as a tom-tom to her.

She and Boris were lucky. Both servants of the Minister left the vast hall by one of the other exits. The Minister was left alone at the ebony table. He rose and opened the top drawer of the ivory cabinet. From it, he drew forth an elaborately carved box inlaid with mother-of-pearl. He took two locks of golden hair from the box and took them to a mirror hanging near the table. He held the locks of hair on either side of his head, pirouetting and chuckling at his reflection.

Boris and Danni crept away from the safety of the curtain and lingered, undecided, in the corridor.

"At least we know where the Grablet is," said Danni.

"But we haven't a clue where to find Webbers," sighed Boris.

"We'll just have to open some doors," Danni said, and she led the way to a branching passage.

They began with the first door they came to. It was

scratched and in need of varnish, but it wasn't locked. Danni opened it cautiously and peeked inside the room. "Only some old furniture," she said, "and it smells of mice." The next room was, disappointingly, the same. And so was the next. And the next, and the one after that. They opened twenty doors in all.

Danni wiggled her little fingers in her ears. She was tired of the horrible Skreek music. It grated on her nerves and seemed to be louder.

They came to the end of the passage. Colossal, battleship-grey metal doors towered in front of them. Boris stared at the great bolt securing the doors. He raised his eyebrows at Danni.

Danni shrugged. "We've come this far. I suppose we might as well look in there too."

Muscles bulging, Boris yanked at the great bolt. It slid, buttery smooth in its socket. He eased the doors open. Just a fraction.

The hideous racket of the Skreek bounded out and washed over them like a pack of hungry wolves, baying, snarling, howling over, around and inside every fibre of their bodies.

A tendril of mist wormed its way along the edge of the door towards Boris. Danni's scream was lost in the devilish din. Her lips snapped together woodenly, like a ventriloquist's dummy.

Boris saw the tendril. Frantically banging shut the steel doors, but without shooting home the bolt, he grabbed Danni's hand and they fled down the passage. They didn't stop until the horrible noise was just a background hum as it had been before.

Danni propped herself against the wall. "I can't go any further," she panted, "my legs have gone to jelly."

"Speaking of legs . . ." Boris stared down the corridor. A tiny boot on the end of a stumpy leg was just appearing round a distant bend. "Isn't that Skive?"

Danni had already wrenched open the nearest door. They staggered into a room and turned the key in the lock. Trying to stop panting, telling her heart to be quiet, Danni listened at the door. She heard soft footsteps. They paused outside the door.

Danni gripped the doorknob. Boris unsheathed his knife.

Skive sniffed. He sniffed again. Danni no longer had to worry about her heart — it almost stopped beating. She heard Skive blow his nose and the whirring of his ear.

The footsteps passed softly away up the passage.

"Phew! He's gone!"

Boris wiped his forehead. "What's he doing back here? He's supposed to be searching for us in The Waste."

"I'm too tired to think," said Danni. "I'm only glad he's got a cold and earache." She collapsed on an ancient bed surrounded by tattered curtains. Boris dropped into a chair next to the bed. They slept for a long time.

When Danni woke, it took a few moments to remember where she was. I'm in the Dreaded Towers with Boris, looking for Webbers. I have to find him soon, she thought. I expect the mould is growing like mad. The Flizzard can probably smell me and what if . . . What's that! She clutched at the bedcover. Something was bending over her.

It was only Boris. "We took the wrong direction," he said. "Right up to the Skreek, no less! We could wander around the Towers forever and never find Webbers. I suggest we contact those men on roller skates and see if they know where he is."

"If we can find them again! Perhaps they'll give us something to eat too."

"I believe these passages wind in circles," said Boris. "If we continue along this one we should find a connection leading to the kitchen corridor." He unlocked the door and peered out to make quite certain the passage was clear before they left the room.

Boris was right. They eventually found a door which led not into a room but into a connecting corridor. Soon they were once again standing in front of the kitchen door, which was still ajar.

Together, they marched into the kitchen and stood side by side, met by the astounded gazes of five men on roller skates.

Boris nodded curtly. "How do you do?" he said. "My companion and I are searching for our friend. He is dressed in black, has long golden hair and webbed feet. Can you help us?"

The five men looked down and studied the feet of Danni and Boris. Danni felt silly with only one foot in a sock and the other bare in her sandal.

Finally, one of the men spoke. His voice was halting and full of wonder. "You came here by yourselves? You weren't brought by the Skreek?"

"Correct!" said Boris.

"Please can you help us?" pleaded Danni. "Would you have any idea where our friend Webbers is? Also, I hate to mention this, but we're very hungry." She looked appealingly at the roller skaters and pointed to her mouth.

"There's nothing left," said one.

"Then do you know where Webbers is kept? Perhaps, if we could find him, we could all help each other to get out of the Dreaded Towers." She tried not to look at the roller skates.

Wistfully, the man repeated after her: "To get out of the Dreaded Towers!" And he looked at the space where his toes should have been.

After yet another long silence, a tall man with an exceptionally elongated and unhappy face said grudgingly, "I think I know where he is."

"Where?" asked Danni.

"Show us!" said Boris.

The man wiped his eye. "Well . . . I'd like to, but I'm

very tired after all this high-speed roller skating and, you see, it's our rest period now before we collect more shrimps from the cellar. It's freezing down there and my arthritis plays up something awful. Then we have to start more cooking and serving. And I have rather bad stomach trouble." He clutched at his stomach and bent over. "I hate curry. The smell fair turns me over. Also, for the last few months I've been suffering from twinges in the neck and, to tell the truth, my kidneys have been . . ."

"That's enough!" interrupted Boris. "We're anxious to find our friend and get him out of this place as soon as possible."

"Well, well! Full marks for manners!" sniffed the long-faced skater. He looked extremely put out. Turning his back, he skated behind the oven and gave a loud and mournful sigh.

Danni hurried after him. "What exactly is wrong with your kidneys?" she asked him kindly. "My Aunt Ricky had the most awful kidney trouble for years until she discovered this marvellous medicine to relieve the pain. Perhaps I can help you?" As she spoke, she took the man's arm and gently but firmly rolled him to the kitchen door.

He responded to her offer with a grey invalid smile on his long, grey face. "Well, you see Miss, it all started when . . ."

"How interesting," said Danni, smiling sweetly. "Now, do we turn left or right?"

"Right. As I was saying, it started with a pain low down in my back . . ."

"Fascinating! Talking about backs, do you think you could give me a piggyback? We could go faster then. Please tell me more about your troubles."

"Up you get. Now, the back is always the first place. I say, can you hear me up there?"

"Is there much further to go? Dreadful thing, kidney trouble."

By this time, they had reached the connecting door to

another passage and were travelling upwards in a gentle spiral. Danni guessed they were headed for one of the seven towers.

Boris was far behind, sprinting to try and keep up with the roller skater.

The man continued the story about his kidneys, but most of his words were lost in the rumble of the skates. He had to open three doors on the way before he slowed down. ". . . and, you see Miss, that's when I suffer the most."

"That's what?" asked Danni vaguely. She got off his back.

"Suffer!" snapped the skater. He looked at her suspiciously. "You *have* been listening, haven't you?"

"Why, of course! My Aunt Ricky had just the same trouble. Is this the door? Is Webbers in here?" She pointed to a keyhole-shaped door painted canary yellow. It was heavily barred.

"About the medicine . . ." said the skater.

But Danni was already lifting the bars. She pulled open the door and entered the room. It was small and completely round. In the middle, under a hanging brass lamp, was a cinnamon velvet couch. On the couch, swamped in a brilliant emerald cape, sat Webbers. Plates of curried shrimp were set before him and two lovely, dark-haired maidens combed his golden hair.

Despite this luxury, Webbers wore a most miserable expression. His eyes were tightly closed and the corners of his mouth were pointing to his chin, like a U upside down.

"Webbers!" cried Danni.

The miserable face changed in an instant. Webbers' eyelids sprang open. He grinned like a slice of watermelon. "It's you! You're safe! I've been sick with worry!"

Danni ran over and hugged him. "I'm so glad to see you, Webbers."

Heavy feet pounded outside the tower room. Boris

burst in and another happy reunion took place. Boris clapped Webbers so hard on the back that Danni was frightened Webbers would never breathe again.

"So!" said Boris briskly. "We won't waste any more time. We came to rescue you, fearing the worst, but I see you have been surprisingly well looked after." His small eyes roved over the plates of shrimp, the velvet couch, the emerald cape and the two surprised maidens.

"It's not as good as it seems," said Webbers. "When I regained consciousness after being carried here by the Skreek, I found myself locked in this tower. My webs were chained to the floor and my hands were tied together. They still are!"

"We'll soon change that!" said Boris.

"That's not all. The Minister said he would keep me here until my hair grows down to my waist. After that, he plans to c . . . cut it off and make a turban for himself. He's already taken two samples. Two samples of my hair! What does it look like, Danni? I haven't been allowed to look in my mirror."

Danni thought his hair was rather chewed looking at the back, but she hoped Webbers might not be able to see that part. "It looks better than ever," she said brightly.

"He sent these two maidens to comb it every day so it will be in top condition for the cutting ceremony," continued Webbers. "I've never liked anyone else touching my hair!" He wrinkled his nose. "And the Minister also despatched these awful curried things for me to eat."

"Shrimps," said Danni. "They don't look too bad to me."

"The Minister says curried shrimp makes the hair grow," said Webbers.

"It hasn't worked for him," giggled Danni.

"He was furious when I said I didn't eat. He tried to make me swallow. He told these maidens to force my mouth open. Goodness knows what my face looks like with all these strange hands touching it!"

"Your face looks just great," comforted Danni. "And don't worry about these shrimps. I'll finish them off." She piled three curried shrimps into her mouth. "Mm. Nice. Like one Boris? It'll be a change from those plants you always eat."

"No time to eat," said Boris. "We must go now." He lifted the emerald cape from Webbers and untied his manacled hands. Kneeling on the floor, he used his knife to break the cruel chains wound about his friend's webs.

"What a relief," Webbers sighed. He stood up shakily. His poor webs were very crumpled and he spent a few moments flexing them before reaching inside a pocket for his small mirror.

Boris paced the floor. "Please, my friend," he begged. "We must leave before we're discovered."

"We have to rescue the Grablet too," said Danni hurriedly, not wanting Webbers to explore the back of his head. "It's in the Minister's dining hall."

"I'm sorry. We'll go right now. I hope the Grablet hasn't been harmed."

Danni giggled. "It called the Minister 'prune-lip' and it wouldn't stop shrieking. The Minister had to put it away in a drawer." She looked at the two maidens, who hadn't uttered a word all this time. "We're getting out of the Dreaded Towers. Do you want to come too?"

Their eyes grew almost as round as Skive's.

"Make up your minds," urged Danni. "We're leaving now."

They both made peculiar grunting noises and nodded.

"If that means 'yes', then come on," said Danni. She looked at their dainty feet. At least they still had toes.

At the yellow door they passed the man on roller skates,

who had been viewing all the proceedings with doleful face unchanged. He caught hold of Danni. "About that medicine. What is it?"

"Medicine? Oh, yes . . . medicine . . . um . . . my Aunt Ricky found love and was never ill again," mumbled Danni. And she scooted away to join the others already racing down the twisting passage.

The roller skater scratched his head and followed them. "How can I find some of this love?" he called to Danni's retreating back.

Webbers, Boris, Danni, the two maidens and the long-faced skater all burst into the kitchen.

"Gather round," ordered Boris, beckoning the other men on skates. "I want to talk about escaping from here."

While he was talking, Danni and Webbers hurried to the Minister's dining hall. Danni took a quick peek around the brocade curtain. "Phew! No-one here." She ran over to the ivory cabinet and pulled open the middle drawer. It was quite empty. "I'm sure he put the Grablet in this one," she said. She wrenched open another drawer. The Grablet wasn't there. She upended all the drawers in the cabinet. Only the box inlaid with mother-of-pearl fell out. Danni felt it wiser not to mention to Webbers what was inside the box. She kicked it under the cabinet. "The Grablet's gone, Webbers! I'll bet that's why Skive came back. He's the nasty little man who found the Grablet when we crashed. He can hear heartbeats with his funny ear. The Minister sent him into The Waste to search for Boris and me. We'll never find him!"

"We'll scour the desert until we do," said Webbers grimly. "The sooner we leave the better."

Back in the corridor outside the kitchen, Boris was lining up the roller skaters and the maidens. "They all want to escape," he said. "Did you get the Grablet?"

"It wasn't there," explained Danni. "I think Skive sneaked back and stole the Grablet again. Webbers said we'll find him in The Waste."

"Right!" barked Boris. "Line up, everyone! Now, this is my plan . . ."

A terrified shout from the passage behind sent them all spinning.

The Minister was bolting towards them.

The roller skaters and the maidens were ready to flee but Boris stopped them. "Stay! We will stay and fight!" He unsheathed his knife again.

The Minister's fleshy face hung in haggard folds. It was as white as ash. "The Skreek! The Skreek!" he shouted. "It turned on me. Some fool left the doors unbolted. The Skreek has escaped!"

9

THE SKREEK SURPRISES

The corridor echoed with the teeth-jarring screeches and howls of the Skreek.

"Let's go!" yelled Danni.

Before he could issue any more orders, Boris was whisked off his feet and slung between three of the skaters. The other two skaters each took a maiden on their backs and rocketed off down the corridor. Webbers took an extra deep breath, Danni grabbed his loops and they sailed up and away, quickly overtaking even the fastest roller skater.

Left far behind, the Minister struggled. He wheezed and he panted. He tried to go faster but the plum robe caught in his knees, tripping him again and again.

Round and down the long corridors swirled the escaping group, until at last they reached a door leading outside. Webbers opened it. He and Danni flew out, followed below by the skaters and their burdens. Along the grey slate flagging rumbled the skaters. Expertly, they jumped the three broad steps. Down the road they zipped, towards the great wall.

Glancing back, Danni glimpsed the Minister emerging from the Dreaded Towers followed by a dark mist. Tendrils of the mist were reaching for him. She saw the Skreek embrace the Minister and, very faintly, heard a single cry before he was swallowed up and whisked away over the tops of the seven towers. "That's the end of the Minister," she said, as Webbers flew over the wall.

They landed on the soft sausage and Webbers pulled the lever to make the wall fold down. A minute later, Boris, the maidens and the five roller skaters tumbled through the gap and lay panting on the sausage.

"We can't stay here," puffed the long-faced skater. "This is where Skive pounced on me before."

"And me!" said the other four, all together.

"Have you tried escaping before?" asked Danni.

The long-faced skater looked greyer than ever. "One after the other, each of us tried. That's how we lost our toes. Skive took them. He waits here for any of the Minister's slaves who leave the towers. There's no other way through the wall, you see. Can we go now? My heart is all a-flutter and my poor muscles are . . ."

Boris calmed him. "The Minister sent Skive away to search The Waste for Danni and me. Nevertheless, we have to be very careful, as both the Watcher and Skive are roaming free. Also, the Skreek is on the loose. For some reason, it no longer wants to be controlled by the Minister and that makes it doubly dangerous!"

"We'd better get to the stone shelter," said Danni, leading the way by jumping off the sausage. The skaters followed but were soon in trouble. Their roller skates bogged in the sand. One of the maidens grunted. She pointed to a speck far away in the sky.

"The Watcher of The Waste!" cried a skater.

"Everyone help!" ordered Boris.

Webbers, Boris, Danni and the maidens pushed and pulled at the skaters, half-dragging them to the shelter. They all squashed in and were very uncomfortable.

"Good gracious! Be careful of my knees," complained the long-faced skater. "They've been very swollen lately." This remark was addressed to one of the maidens who was pressed up against him.

The maiden smiled shyly and blushed baby-pink.

Danni noticed the skater change colour. He turned from grey to a salmon shade. And was that a tiny crack of a smile?

He spoke again to the maiden, this time in a more friendly tone. "You have very nice teeth. You know, I suffer dreadfully from toothache but, strangely, it seems to have gone today."

"Quiet!" whispered Boris.

A shadow flitted across the sand.

Everyone stiffened. An uneasy silence hovered over them. Faces shone with perspiration, joints ached, limbs went numb. Boris could take it no longer. Crouching low, he crept from the shelter.

Danni saw Webbers trying to follow. Unfortunately, his web was pinned by a skate. Ignoring his warning look, she ducked under the nearest pair of legs and stole after Boris, following in his stalking footsteps.

Suddenly, a figure bounded from behind a stone.

Danni screamed, but Boris only barked out a short laugh. "Ha! Aren't you one of the gardeners from the West Field?"

"Very glad to see you, sir," replied the gardener. "I heard voices in that there pile of stones and was sneaking up to see who it was."

"What happened to you and the others?" asked Danni. "Where are the cups?"

The gardener took a breath. "Well, in all that darkness it was hard to see and that Watcher thing was wriggling around confusing us. We went off in the wrong direction — ended up going in circles. In the morning, we found the wall and saw the wreckage of your cup. We went back to The Poles to collect more searchers, though we didn't think there was much of a chance of finding you in all this Waste even if the Skreek and the rest of whatever is in them towers hadn't got you first." He sighed, exhausted by his long speech.

"Where are the others?" asked Boris.

"There are three cups searching hereabouts. I'll call them from my cup." And the gardener strode off.

Boris stroked his long nose. "The skaters will have to go first. And the maidens. You could fit in too, Danni, but I'll have to wait for another cup."

"I'll go with Webbers," said Danni, "but we'll wait with you."

Soon the other cups arrived and the five skaters and one maiden squeezed in. The other maiden stood looking forlornly at the others.

"Couldn't she sit on my knee?" suggested the long-faced skater.

"I thought you had swollen knees," said Danni.

The skater glared at her. "I did. But they're much better now."

Danni giggled. So did Webbers. So did the other skaters and both the maidens. They had all escaped from the Dreaded Towers and were just beginning to realise it. Even the long-faced skater, after turning an even deeper salmon shade, gave a rusty cackle. "Hee, hee . . . creak . . . hee, hee."

Boris lifted the maiden onto the skater's knee. Before the cups took off, Danni asked her, "How come Skive didn't take your toes?"

One of the skaters replied. "I'm sorry to say the maiden's toes weren't big enough. Skive took their tongues instead."

Danni's knees wobbled. "All this time I was worrying about my toes and I could have lost my tongue!"

The long-faced skater leaned over the side of the cup and whispered, "I think I've found some of that medicine."

As the cups rose slowly upward, Danni just caught the skater's words to the maiden on his knee. "I shall be your tongue and you shall be my toes. Together, we shall never be ill again. I have it on the best authority from Danni's Aunt Ricky."

The three who were left behind moved back into the stone shelter to wait for another cup.

Soon, Danni saw a shadow pass over the desert floor. "Hurrah! Here's our cup!" she cried, and joyfully raced out of the shelter.

She was much too hasty. In one frightful second a feeler with a grip of iron shot from a tight, coppery robe and clutched her neck. There she was, staring face to horrible hood with the Watcher of The Waste!

Danni struggled with all her might but, in the grip of the Watcher, she was as feeble as a rabbit in a trap. Webbers and Boris rushed to help her. Boris caught the Watcher's neck. Webbers dived for her middle. The Watcher's narrow body pulsed and vibrated, slithering through their hands like an eel.

Then the sinister figure twirled, tossing all three to the sand where they sprawled on their bellies.

Evilly, triumphantly, the Watcher laughed. "You fools! The Minister's servant will see to you all!" And she thrust her feeler towards the sky.

Danni spat sand. She mumbled, "But the Minister isn't here any more. He was taken."

The Watcher cackled. "Ark, ark, ark. Taken? Nonsense! You are the ones who will be taken." She clapped her feelers together and the copper robe rustled like a shroud.

Then they all heard the dreadful music of the Skreek. They saw its murky, ominous shape. It was dropping towards them.

"You and Danni go!" Boris yelled at Webbers. "Leave me!"

There was no time. Tendrils of the hideous mist reached down. The noise was an appalling alley-cats' chorus. It tore at their eardrums. Senses reeled as all sane thought fled from their minds.

The Watcher of The Waste looked on mercilessly. "Ark, ark, ark, ark, ar . . . arr . . .? What . . .?"

Open-mouthed, Danni goggled as the Skreek wrapped itself around the Watcher!

"Not me, you idiot!" she snarled, and pointed at the three sprawled on the sand. "Down there! Get them! What do you think you're d . . .?" She fainted in the grip of the terrible mist.

Clasping its prize, the Skreek scudded away in the direction in which it had taken the Minister.

"I can't believe it!" Webbers rose and flicked sand from his black tube.

"Perhaps the Skreek isn't so bad after all, except for that awful noise it makes," said Danni.

"It seems to have changed its mind about who its friends are," agreed Boris. He pointed over the desert. "Hey! There's one . . . no, two cups arriving! Both of you can travel in style for a change."

As soon as the two vehicles landed, Boris jumped into one and Danni into the other. "Come on, Webbers," called Danni. "It's not so bad in one of these."

Webbers looked at the cup as a racehorse might look at a hack. "I suppose it won't do any harm," he sniffed, and got in most haughtily. The driver inspected Webbers very closely. His tiny eyes travelled from top to bottom, lingering on the webs. "Been to a fancy dress?" he asked. "Didn't know they went in for such light entertainment in the Dreaded Towers. Nice piece of work, those paper flappers on your feet."

Webbers looked like he'd swallowed a worm. Danni burst out laughing. After a moment, Webbers joined in and the whole cup shivered with their merriment.

"Tut, tut, the poor things," wailed the driver. "They've been out here too long. Their minds are addled."

When he stopped laughing, Webbers remembered to ask the driver to fly low over the desert so they could search for Skive.

The two cups flew close together, zigzagging over The Waste for a long time. It was Danni who first pointed to something far away on the sandy horizon.

"That's only a rain cloud," said the driver.

"That's not what I mean. Look under it," said Danni.

"Yes, I see it too," said Webbers. He shouted to Boris and the two cups forged ahead until they circled a round, green ball dozing on a sand dune.

The ball rolled over and stared up at them.

"That's Skive!" cried Danni. She poked her head over the side of the cup. "We know you've got the Grablet. You'd better hand it over!"

Skive snarled up at Danni. He shook his baby fist. "Naaaooowww!" His ear began to turn and he scrambled to his feet, staring at Danni through eyes which had turned very hungry-looking.

The cups landed. Boris and Webbers sprang out to capture Skive, but the little man bristled. His teeth seemed to grow longer and sharper as he gnashed and clashed them together like iron gates each time Boris or Webbers stepped closer.

"Give me the Grablet," said Webbers.

"Grrr," snarled Skive and snapped at Webbers' bare arm. "It's mine. I found it!"

"Only by accident," said Boris. "We've come to get it back!"

"Grrr," snarled Skive again, clashing perilously close to Boris's knee. "I won't!"

I'll have to help, thought Danni. They'll never get close enough to grab Skive. She started to get out of the cup but the driver held her back.

"Look!" he said, staring up. "What's that?"

The small rain cloud, high above, had turned into an

arrow. And the arrow was hurtling down towards them like a pitch black bolt of lightning.

It came so quickly, so quietly, that Boris and Webbers never saw it coming. Nor did Skive. Danni only had a second in which to pray that she wasn't the target before the arrow sped right through Skive, piercing his chest and pinning him to the sand dune.

The black arrow twisted and turned, lost its shape, puffed out and grew cloudy.

"My, my," gasped the driver of the cup. "That's the Skreek!"

"You're right," whispered Danni. "Who would have thought it could do what it just did?"

Swiftly imprisoning Skive, the Skreek resumed its ghastly music and raised the little fellow from the sand dune.

"Hang on, Skreek! Just a second! Don't take Skive just yet!" cried Danni. "He's still got the Grablet. Please, please, let us have the Grablet before you take Skive away!"

The Skreek hesitated. It moved slowly over Danni's cup and there it hovered. Danni plugged her ears, for so loud, so terrible was the Skreek music it made her head bubble like a pot of stew.

The Skreek's tendrils writhed. Danni saw Skive turned about, upended and shaken like a sauce bottle which hasn't much left in the bottom.

A tin dropped from the neck of Skive's jumper and landed at Danni's feet. Before Danni had time to say thank you, the Skreek scudded away with its victim.

Danni snatched up the tin and tore off the lid. A feeble voice quavered, "About time too!"

10

BACK
TO THE
POLES

"Hi, Grablet!"

"Is that you, Danni?"

"Yes, it's me. And Webbers is here too, and Boris."

"I never thought I'd see you again. Take me out, please."

Danni noticed that some of the Grablet's holes were a little frayed around the edges.

"It'll take me a long time to get over this!" gasped the Grablet. "I have been confined in a hot and smelly tin. I was stolen by a repulsive, sniffling creature with a mad ear and scary teeth. A creature who said he'd keep me forever in a marble crypt chanting to toe bones. Toe bones, I tell you! And a crypt, of all things! You know how I love fresh air and breezes!" A couple of the holes gaped loosely and quivered.

"Well, his nasty plan has been foiled," said Boris, who had come over with Webbers. "The Skreek made short work of that evil little object!"

"What's been happening to you?" asked the Grablet in a stronger voice.

"We'll tell you everything on the way back to The Poles," said Danni.

Danni and Webbers took it in turns to tell the Grablet about their adventures in the Dreaded Towers. It was hard to tell whether the Grablet or the driver of the cup was the more amazed.

Eventually, the Grablet dozed off in Danni's hand, worn out by excitement.

Webbers yawned. "I hope we get to Boris's place soon. I'm not used to being carried like this."

"Boris's people live in balloons," said Danni. "I wonder why?"

"To save more space on the ground, of course," explained the driver. "For more plants."

During their journey back, Danni thought of the skaters. "Those poor men without toes," she said sadly, "and those two lovely maidens without tongues. I feel so sorry for them."

Webbers nodded. "We also have to think about *your* problem again. Can't afford to lose any more time. Have you noticed an increase in the mould?"

"There hasn't been a moment to look. But at least I still have my toes — those men have lost theirs forever."

"I'll see what I can do about their troubles," said Webbers, taking out his comb.

"How? How will you see about them? Have you got something from NITT to help them get around better than those skates?"

"Not exactly."

"A cure then, like mine?"

"Sort of, but not quite."

"Tell me! Please, Webbers."

Webbers put down his comb and went through his pockets. He turned out a number of interesting things, including a bubble-pipe, a stick of charcoal, an ivory elephant and a squashed lady bug before announcing, "This is it. I wonder if they still work." In his hand was the little book Danni had seen once before. The biscuit-coloured cover was worn, its corners rounded and dog-eared with age.

"How can you help them with just that little book?" scoffed Danni.

"Have a look," said Webbers, "but be careful. I can never get another copy. That's the only one in existence."

Danni could just make out the title, stamped into the leather cover. It was "RESTORATIONS". She opened the book. On the flyleaf, in spidery, faded handwriting, was written: *Property of Martinoss Hep*. The entire book was written in the same spidery hand and contained strange rhymes and instructions. All the rhymes dealt with parts of the body. Danni looked at the section on toes. "There's nothing about mould from a Moldy Flizzard's egg," she said.

"No. Old Martinoss didn't concern himself with that sort of problem. The book deals with items either missing or disarranged through no fault of the person or creature concerned."

"Where did you get it? Who is Martinoss?"

"The book came from Martinoss Hep himself, distinguished sage and founder of the New Ideas Testing Team. He was a very old man when I joined NITT and, before he died, he bequeathed to me his restoration recipes, gathered over a lifetime. I've never used them."

Danni found a rhyme about ears. "Hear ye, hear ye, Angel of the Ear . . ."

"No!" Webbers' hand bolted across and seized her wrist. "You must never utter lightly anything in that book. You're likely to end up with something you never bargained for." Taking the book from her, he opened the back page and read:

> *If unbidden you seek to borrow,*
> *A rhyme compiled by me, Martinoss,*
> *You shall find to your great sorrow,*
> *A peculiar addition, or another loss.*

"A peculiar addition, or another loss," repeated Danni. "I

don't like the sound of that! I've already got a peculiar addition and I don't want to lose anything — like the skaters and the maidens. I promise I won't say any of those rhymes!"

"Good girl. Just leave it to me."

At dusk, they reached the end of The Waste. Danni pointed below to the bobbing plants. "We must remember to put 'a fresh and tender leaf' into the purple water."

"First thing in the morning," promised Webbers.

It was the middle of the night when they reached The Poles, but a tremendous crowd waited to cheer them. Boris was greeted first by an old man whom Danni recognised as having attended to the two men who had been in the crashed cup at the start of the journey.

"This is Old Wen," Boris told Webbers. "I suggest we three get together and discuss what we've found out about the Dreaded Towers."

They climbed the metal ladder to Boris's balloon. The trapdoor was opened by Beta. Boris half-smiled at Danni. "This time, I insist you do as I say and go with Beta. Have a good, long sleep, my friend."

Danni didn't argue. She followed Beta behind a chequered blue and yellow wallhanging. On the other side was heaped a pile of light, spongy fibres which made a comfortable-looking bed. But better than the bed was what stood next to it — a tub of steaming water.

When Beta left her, Danni carefully laid the sleeping Grablet on the bed and undressed. She left the striped sock until last.

Trying hard to think of the skaters who were far worse off, Danni slowly rolled it down. She discovered a small hole in the heel and instantly felt sick. When had it happened? How long had the mould smell been escaping? When would the Moldy Flizzard arrive to claim her?

Danni closed her eyes as the sock peeled away from her toes. Her stomach heaved and she tasted something bitter as the foulest smell of the filthiest drain rose into her nostrils.

Making a big effort, she prised open one eyelid and glared savagely at her big toe. She had expected the mould to have grown. But it was a shock to see just how much. The mould had completely covered her big toe in a shiny cap of fungus. That wasn't all. Its searching fingers had spread to her second toe, had swallowed up the space next to her third toe, had crawled across to her fourth and were now marching towards her baby toe.

Danni stuffed her fist in her mouth to keep from crying out. She told herself to calm down, to think, Danni, think.

When she'd stopped trembling, she pulled a stringy fibre from her bed, threaded it around the hole in the sock and pulled the hole closed. She tied the ends of the fibre tightly, and quickly put the sock on so she wouldn't have to see the mould — or worse, smell it!

Keeping her right leg clear of the water, Danni hopped on one leg into the tub and bathed herself. A great weariness washed over her with the soothing water. When she hopped out, she was more than ready for the spongy bed, and soon joined the snoring Grablet.

Danni's mouth was dry as dust when she woke. She was grateful for the mug of thick, green liquid which Beta brought, and drank it down in four big gulps.

When she was dressed, Webbers peered around the wallhanging. "Glad you're up," he said. "Have you checked on the . . .?"

"It's grown all over my toes now," said Danni, waggling her foot at him. "There was a hole in the sock but I mended it last night. Can you smell anything?"

Webbers sniffed. "Not much, but I bet it's stronger than a satellite beam to a Moldy Flizzard. Why didn't you tell me last night? We could have left straight away."

"Where's the Grablet?" Danni asked, changing the subject. "It was next to my head last night."

"With Old Wen and Boris. We were up most of the night talking about the Dreaded Towers and discussing ways to help the people of Bearakha." Webbers frowned. "We can't stay and help now. Your problem is the more urgent one!"

"But what about the skaters and maidens? We can't just go off without trying RESTORATIONS!"

"The Moldy Flizzard could turn up at any moment," warned Webbers.

Danni hopped from one foot to the other. She sucked in her cheeks. It was a terrible decision to make. She thought of the mould sprinting over her foot, thought of herself smelling worse than a dead rat, thought of being hugged by the Moldy Flizzard and of disappearing into its pouch . . . and said, in a small voice: "We should stay here and help first."

Webbers sighed. He ran his hand over his forehead and down his cheek. "Let's do it quickly. Come on!"

Danni found Boris and Old Wen seated on the floor of the balloon surrounded by notes. The Grablet was perched on Old Wen's head. "Did you have a bath?" it inquired.

"None of your business!" retorted Danni.

"I only thought you smelled a bit," said the Grablet.

"Why are you always so rude?"

"Me? I'm not . . ."

"Quiet!" commanded Webbers. He looked down at Boris and Old Wen. "We have to leave Bearakha as soon as we can, but before we do I'd like to try and help the skaters who have lost their toes and the maidens who have lost their tongues."

"Aren't you staying?" Boris sprang to his feet. "What about our plans? I thought you'd come on our next expedition to the Dreaded Towers. I want to find out what the Skreek did with the Minister and the Watcher and Skive. I want to find out how the Minister obtained those shrimps when we've had nothing but the plant to eat for so long, and whether there's anyone else locked in the towers and . . ."

"I won't be coming. Not this time," said Webbers. "Sometime, I'll visit Bearakha again. In the meantime . . . whoops!"

Webbers lost his balance. A sudden, fierce wind had sprung up. The balloon slewed crazily, first this way, then the other. They heard a blizzard-like howling and a fearful commotion going on outside, a hubbub of voices raised in alarm. Over and above those noises came the shriek and wail of discordant notes.

"The Skreek!" yelled Danni. "The Skreek's out there!"

"It's never been right up to The Poles before," quaked Old Wen.

Reeling with the balloon, Boris tottered to the trapdoor and wrenched it open. He disappeared down the ladder, tagged by Old Wen and Webbers. Pausing to pick up the Grablet which had been tossed from Old Wen's head, Danni followed.

Once outside, she understood the reason for the commotion. In the fields of lilac flowers, the men, women and children of the settlement were gathered, heads craned upward, watching a sight to make anyone yell with fear.

The Skreek was locked in combat with the Moldy Flizzard.

Billowing like the sails of a storm-tossed schooner, the wings of the Moldy Flizzard flapped up face-slapping blasts of wind.

Murky tendrils twisting and writhing, the Skreek wailed its hellish music and attempted to grip the giant, scaly bulk of the Moldy Flizzard.

Two mighty forces had met in battle. Danni held her breath. Which one would win? She didn't want to be captured by the Moldy Flizzard, yet she didn't want the creature to be hurt either.

Higher and louder rose the noise of the Skreek, the discords vibrating the balloons and making them twang like rubber bands. The people of Bearakha held their hands to their hound-like ears, trying to block out the noises which threatened to burst their eardrums.

"It's horrible! Like music played backwards!" shouted Danni. She had to put the Grablet in her pocket so she, too, could plug up her ears.

The next moment, the Moldy Flizzard sagged. Its massive body slipped closer to the ground. Its wings drooped like sodden, wrinkled curtains. The ground of Bearakha quaked as the Moldy Flizzard crashed with a mighty *thwumpa!*

The Skreek hummed and hovered over the Flizzard. Six dozen tendrils reached around the great creature. But the Moldy Flizzard was much too big, much too heavy for the Skreek to lift.

Danni plucked at Webbers' arm. Her eyes brimmed. "The Moldy Flizzard isn't dead, is it?" she sobbed.

11

RARE RHYMES

"The Flizzard is just unconscious," replied Webbers. "The Skreek doesn't kill, but its noise can knock you out better than a rock dropped on your head. The poor old Moldy Flizzard will probably be stunned for a while. It'll be interesting to see what the Skreek does now."

Danni was poised to run up the ladder of the nearest balloon. However, it didn't look as if the Skreek intended to move in her direction — or in anyone else's. It hovered over the still form of the Moldy Flizzard as if on guard, humming in a frightening sort of way.

Webbers looked very thoughtful. "What did you say before, Danni?"

"When?"

"Just before the Moldy Flizzard fell. Something about music."

"I said the Skreek noises are like music played backwards."

"Mm. That's given me an idea." Webbers searched through his pockets. He found a carved wooden bull, a cap made of wire, seven fancy corks and an acid drop before he pulled out a squashy thing that looked like an overstuffed mosquito with teeth. "NITT asked me to test this silly-looking thing ages ago."

It was about the length of a pen and as wide as Danni's

fingers held together. She poked it. It felt soft as dough. "What's it called?"

"A Musical Mozzy. Can you play any sort of instrument?"

Danni shook her head. "*That's* an instrument?"

"I can't play anything either," said Webbers, turning hopefully to Boris.

"Nor can I," said Boris, "but Old Wen can play the violin."

Old Wen stared in bewilderment at the Musical Mozzy. "It doesn't look a bit like a violin," he muttered.

"The Skreek may be asking for help," said Webbers. "It's come right to The Poles and yet it's not trying to take away any more people. Perhaps it wants to play music properly." He held the Musical Mozzy out to Old Wen. "Try tucking it under your arm."

"What do I do then?" asked Old Wen.

"Afraid I don't know. I never learned to play an instrument."

Old Wen squeezed the squashy part of the Musical Mozzy. A heavenly note issued from it. Old Wen pressed one of its buck teeth and the note hung in the air like the sweetest perfume.

"That's marvellous!" encouraged Danni.

Old Wen did a few more squeezes and a few more twiddles on the shiny teeth, then he smiled at Danni. "I'll give it a go," he said.

Advancing bravely towards the Skreek, he stopped two metres from the body of the Moldy Flizzard, tucked the Musical Mozzy under his left arm and began to play. At first, the Mozzy's notes were drowned out by the Skreek. Old Wen kept practising and after ten minutes Danni noticed a difference in the Skreek's sounds. They weren't so loud and they weren't so frightening.

Having mastered the Musical Mozzy, the old man played a lilting air. The Skreek hummed brokenly, trying to follow the air. Five or six times Old Wen played the same tune, until the Skreek copied it note for note. The Musical Mozzy soared like a bird in spring. The Skreek did the same. The Mozzy changed tempo and sang with wild, exciting gypsy music.

"Old Wen can really play!" shouted Danni.

"Like an angel!" cried Webbers.

The Skreek copied the gypsy music, swirling and twirling as the music became wilder. Then Old Wen made the Musical Mozzy play a delightful rhapsody. The Skreek followed every note.

"The Musical Mozzy has taught the Skreek to play in tune," Danni chuckled. "The Skreek loves it!"

"Notice anything else?" asked Webbers.

"Yes! The Skreek is changing colour. It's turning white!"

"Wish I could see," grumbled the Grablet from inside Danni's pocket.

"The Skreek isn't dark any more," explained Danni. "It looks like a fluffy white cloud. And it's doing everything the Mozzy does, except it sounds even better!"

"There's nothing wrong with my hearing," growled the Grablet.

The Skreek was making up its own little frills to the musical piece. It sounded like a choir of cherubs singing, whereas the Musical Mozzy now sounded rather thin. Danni thought she heard it play a few wrong chords. Its heavenly notes changed to squeaks, and a tooth fell out.

Old Wen dropped the Musical Mozzy but the Skreek continued to play superbly on its own.

Danni took the Grablet from her pocket. "It worked," she said, and ran over to inspect the Mozzy. It lay like an exhausted glove. "The Musical Mozzy is all washed up," she called to Webbers.

Webbers scribbled a note on his NITT notepad. "It served a purpose," he said, "but NITT will have to make sure future Mozzies are much stronger."

Old Wen called for silence. When everyone had stopped chattering, all faces turned towards Webbers. Old Wen stood as tall as he could and held his arms out to Webbers.

The people of Bearakha cheered and applauded.

"Make way!" someone shouted. Hanging on to anyone who was close, pushing awkwardly through the crowd, came four of the skaters rescued from the Dreaded Towers. Behind them scurried one of the maidens.

"That was a miracle," said a skater, shaking Webbers' hand vigorously. The other skaters copied him. Webbers' arm went up and down like a piston.

"Danni gave me the idea." Webbers hastily hid his arms behind his back. "And Old Wen is a great musician."

"Pity you couldn't do something about our toes," said one skater glumly. "We can't do our work in the gardens any more. The skates get caught in the roots of the plants."

"Webbers can help you," Danni announced.

The skaters' mouths dropped open in surprise.

"Just a minute," said Webbers. "I don't know if I can, I just said I'd try."

The skaters closed their mouths. The maiden tugged at Webbers' arm. She pleaded with her eyes.

"Yes," piped up the Grablet, "you too, my dear."

"Could you make us a private shelter? Here on the ground?" Webbers asked Boris. "I'm sorry to spoil more of your plants. The Moldy Flizzard has already squashed a great many of them."

"A small price to pay for what you've done," said Boris. He directed his men to build a tent. After much scurrying up and down balloons, the men erected a tent out of broom handles and woven rugs.

"We can't start yet," said Danni. "Where is the long-faced skater? You know, the one who was always sick. And where is the other maiden?"

"They married as soon as we got back to The Poles and we haven't seen them since," explained a skater.

A search party was immediately despatched to try and find them.

Flares were lit around the tent. Inside, Webbers sat in a circle drawn on cleared ground. The four skaters lay full length around the circle, feet pointing towards Webbers. Their skates had been removed and were being held by Old Wen. The maiden was watching from a corner, the Grablet perched on her shoulder.

Still there was no sign of the missing couple.

Webbers clicked his tongue. "I can't wait. Everything is ready." Taking up RESTORATIONS, he turned to a page he'd marked with a leaf, cleared his throat and, in a strong, clear voice, read:

> There came four Lords out of the West,
> One bore pitch and one bore coffee,
> These were black and, as for the rest,
> One bore toes and the other, toffee,
> These were pale and the Heavens can tell,
> One of them we need so well.
> So go away pitch and go away coffee,
> We don't need you and we don't want toffee,
> Speaking now to One who knows,
> Lord of the West, leave your TOES!

Coming from outside the tent, Danni heard sounds of marching footsteps. The flares, which could be seen through the woven rugs, stopped flickering. An eerie stillness gripped the air.

The marching sounds entered the tent, right next to where Danni stood. The sounds marched through the tent and around the circle scratched in the ground. They paused at each skater in turn. Each time there was a pause, the skater shuddered deeply and mewed like a kitten. Then the sounds marched out of the tent. The flares flickered once more, the skaters lay stretched stiff as planks and the silence was unbroken.

Webbers looked up from the book. He rose and carefully stepped over the circle. Drawing Boris and Old Wen together, he said, "By the time I've told the rhyme for the maiden's tongue, we'll be able to see if Martinoss's recipes work. Even if the rhyme has worked, it will be two days before the skaters' toes have been fully restored. Will you see that they lie here undisturbed?"

"Of course," replied Old Wen, "but what about that creature outside? Won't it disturb the lot of us when it wakes up? Will it go on a rampage and destroy us all?"

"No, it won't harm a single one of you. We'll be gone from Bearakha and it will follow us."

"What about the married couple?" said Boris. "Can you leave the rhyme for me to say?"

"No, I can't. The power was given to me alone."

Danni retrieved the Grablet from the maiden's shoulder.

"Please help the maiden, Danni," Webbers instructed. "Seat her comfortably in that corner by herself."

When Danni had arranged the maiden cross-legged on the ground, Webbers read the appropriate page in RESTORATIONS. He got Boris to cut some plant stems, then he arranged the stems in a little fence in front of the maiden. He took a silk handkerchief from a pocket and opened the book again.

Danni peeked at the title of the rhyme. It was: "Tongues, Unmarried Females".

Webbers began:

> Queen of the Mouth,
> From your home in the South,
> I ask you to bring your sweet touch.
> The object mislaid,
> (Through no fault of this maid)
> Is her tongue, which she needs very much.
> If you help to restore,
> Her speech organ once more,

Great praise she shall give unto you.
The maid will give voice,
And we all shall rejoice,
That her tongue has been fashioned anew.

From the top of the tent came a whirr of wings. Startled, Danni looked up, but saw nothing. The sound of a glorious bird call was repeated three times. It made Danni feel happy, and she smiled. She noticed that Boris and Old Wen were smiling too, and she heard the Grablet chuckling.

The maiden's head suddenly flopped backwards. Her lips yawned wide, then snapped together like a clam shell. The whirr of wings and a final birdcall sounded, and the tent was perfectly quiet again.

Webbers tied the handkerchief around the lower half of the maiden's face. "She must not try to speak for one whole day," he explained to Boris. "After that, she must practise as much as possible."

Above the handkerchief, the maiden's green eyes looked gratefully at Webbers. Danni kissed her on the forehead. "Goodbye. I'm sure your tongue will be back to normal soon."

"Farewell, my dear," crooned the Grablet.

They examined the skaters. The men were sitting up, gazing at their feet and sighing with pleasure. On the ends of their feet were the tiny beginnings of pale toes.

Webbers picked up Danni and swung her high in the air.

"Hurrah for Webbers! Hurrah for Danni! Hurrah for Boris!" shouted the erstwhile skaters.

"Don't forget me. Hurrah for the Grablet!" shouted the Grablet.

As they left the tent, a messenger hurried up, carrying a note from the long-faced skater. The note thanked them all (especially Danni's Aunt Ricky) for everything they had done. It said that he and his wife were happy as they were and did not want back his toes or her tongue.

"If they change their minds they can tell me when I next visit Bearakha," said Webbers.

"Please make it soon," said Boris. He had assembled the entire population of The Poles to say goodbye. Even the newly whitened Skreek hovered around, playing a heartrending farewell tune.

Danni cautiously examined the Moldy Flizzard. It still lay motionless. She couldn't see even one eyelash flickering. "It won't harm any of you when it wakes up," she assured Boris. "It only wants me."

Boris gazed at her solemnly. "You have been a fine, brave companion, Danni, and I shall always remember you. I hope you find whatever it is you seek."

"That reminds me," said Danni, plucking a fresh green leaf from the nearest plant. She held it out to Webbers who found the jar, unscrewed the lid and dropped the leaf in the purple water.

Boris turned his attention to the Grablet. "As for you, Grablet, I didn't have time to get to know you well, but perhaps we'll have the pleasure of meeting again some day. In the meantime," he faltered and his weeny eyes turned misty, "I ask you to look after Danni."

"Goodbye, Boris," said the Grablet gravely. "I'm sorry I couldn't give you the benefit of my wisdom when you and Danni ventured into the Dreaded Towers. However, you did quite well for amateurs. I'm very glad I didn't end up in a crypt full of toe bones. Not the ideal place for a Grablet of great intelligence. And now, to complete my farewell speech, I propose to chant a going-away ode of deep and haunting beauty which I . . ."

The Grablet couldn't finish because Danni hurriedly zipped it into her pocket. Webbers and Danni both swallowed a yellow Mos tablet and, once again, Danni grasped the shoulder loops on Webbers' black tube.

"Goodbye Boris! Goodbye everyone!" called Danni.

Swiftly, they rose into the air. Beneath them, the crowd cheered and waved. The imposing figure of Boris stood out clearly from the rest but soon he, too, vanished in the distance.

Later, when Danni glanced back, Bearakha resembled a bright, sparkling ball.

Silhouetted against the ball was a winged shadow.

12

QUEEN DANNI

"Go faster!" yelled Danni. "The Moldy Flizzard is following us!"

"What's that?" cried the Grablet. "Flizzard? Great gollops! The Skreek didn't knock it out for long."

Webbers' breathing came deep and fast. *Shoof, shoof, shoof.* He sounded like a steam iron. Now they were hurtling through space faster than a comet. For Danni, all idea of time was lost. She felt as if she was swooping through a dark tunnel, swallowed up by a giant vacuum cleaner. She didn't know how long it was before Webbers slowed down.

"Anything behind us?" he asked.

Danni's neck was stiff from pressing against the black tube. She almost expected it to creak when she turned to look. "Can't see anything," she said.

"That's a relief," said the Grablet. "I might have been hurt if the Flizzard had grabbed you."

"Never mind about *you* being hurt," said Webbers. "What's the next verse? Hurry up Grablet."

The Grablet sniffed. In a low voice, it began: " 'On Sifania's gentle . . .' "

"What? Speak up!" demanded Webbers.

" 'ON SIFANIA'S GENTLE LANDSCAPE,' " boomed the Grablet.

"Not quite as loud as that," said Webbers.
"Make up your mind!

> *On Sifania's gentle landscape,*
> *Find a cube that's ripe and brown,*
> *Give its nectar to the jar,*
> *And shake it up and down."*

"Is that all?" asked Webbers.
"As far as I know!" snapped the Grablet.
"Sifania," said Webbers.
"Do you know where Sifania is?" Danni asked. But Webbers was already making shoofing noises again. He took a swoop to the left and once more they were hurtling through space at an indescribable speed. Time meant nothing, but it seemed to Danni only a few minutes had passed before Webbers slowed down and passed a green Mos tablet over his shoulder.

After swallowing the tablet, Danni felt curiously light. "I feel like a feather," she said dreamily. "I could float away."

"We'd better take another half each," said Webbers. "I feel the same way."

The extra half tablet made Danni feel normal again and she began to take an interest in the planet which had appeared on her right.

Gentle rays from a small sun felt like a warm sponge caressing Danni's body as they landed. "Sifania's beautiful!" she cried. Crystal waters lapped against cliffs of mustard yellow. Trees in the shapes of pears, hearts and clovers were hung with strange fruits such as Danni had never seen before. She took the Grablet from her pocket. "Just look at all those different kinds of fruit," she said. "I'm hungry!"

"Mm," said the Grablet unenthusiastically.

"Can I try some, Webbers?"

Webbers took out the jar of purple water and laid it on the ground. "As many as you like," he said. "I'm going to have a quick dip after that hurried journey." And he dived straight into the clear water and started swimming, his webs becoming paddles to shoot him forward two metres at a time.

"I'd love a swim too," said Danni. She took off her sandals, then remembered she couldn't dive in and join Webbers as it would be impossible to keep her sock dry.

"Foo! There's a bit of a whiff around here that could be you," said the Grablet.

Danni examined the heel of her sock and groaned. "No wonder. The hole's back . . . the fibre has snapped."

"Well, mend the hole!" snapped the Grablet. "It's like waving a flag at the Moldy Flizzard and saying 'come and get me'!"

Cupping her hands, Danni shouted at Webbers. He was splashing far out from the mustard banks but it took only five seconds for those paddling webs to push him back again. He hoisted himself out. "What's up?" Drops of water rolled off his tube as smoothly as they did from Danni's ducks back on Earth.

Danni showed him the hole. "I need some darning wool."

"Should have something here," said Webbers. He opened a couple of pockets and out came a paintbrush, a miniature copper kettle, a lace collar, and a tiny glass casket containing a sugared violet.

"Sorry. They're no use," said Danni.

Webbers yawned. After searching four more pockets, he came up with a packet of needles and a reel of thick, white cotton.

"Thanks. They'll do."

"While you're darning, I'll have a quick snooze." Webbers closed his eyes and leaned backwards. His webs floated up and his wet hair hung down in seaweedy strands. He opened one eye. "To save time, you could get the cube. Make sure it's a ripe brown one."

Danni waited until she was sure Webbers was fast

asleep before unrolling the sock.

"Great gollops! Zincs above! Ber-*lurk*!" gasped the Grablet as her foot was revealed. "Keep it far away from me!"

Danni said nothing. She thought she'd be strong enough by now to look at the mould without shuddering. But still her stomach turned over, and her spine fizzed like bubbles in a spa tub. The mould had become a greeny-grey blanket. It covered all her toes, the top of her foot and her ankle. And there was something else. It was sprouting — buds of the sickly-coloured fungus flowers she had seen on the Moldy Flizzard's egg had pushed up through the mould. They grinned at her like baby toads.

The smell was even worse. Danni retched. Holding back tears, she bit her tongue, promising herself she would not cry in front of the Grablet. Her hand had the tremor of an old lady's as she tried to thread the largest of the needles with heavy cotton. If the Grablet says anything else, she thought, I'll . . . I'll . . .

But the Grablet had enough sense to change the subject. "I can see a brown cube," it said. "There are lots of them hanging on that tree which looks like your mouth when you're thinking."

"What?" Danni looked up. She giggled in spite of herself. "A heart, you mean."

"If you say so," said the Grablet. "I haven't got one."

"What are you, anyway?" asked Danni, darning the sock with big, uneven stitches. "What are you made of?"

The Grablet's holes squeezed together. "Well," it said in a high voice, "I'm unusual, that's a fact. I've never heard of anything else quite like me. I don't think I had a mother and a father — at least I've never met them. And I definitely don't have brothers and sisters. That makes me rather special, doesn't it? I named myself, of course. And I'm made of Grabletstuff. It's not like your skin — it's much tougher, and has a beautiful sheen, don't you think?"

"Now that I've got used to looking at you, I think you're quite nice," replied Danni. "Also, you're very easy to cart around and you don't cost any money to feed." She finished darning the hole and put on the sock. The smell disappeared. "Let's get the cube," she said. "Then I'm going to try lots of those different fruits."

Carrying the jar, she walked over to the heart-shaped tree and found a plump cube. "This looks just right." She plucked it and squeezed the juice into the jar, which she then shook vigorously. The purple water turned a deeper shade.

Danni plucked another brown cube and ate it. "Delicious! Like a summer strawberry," she said. "Pity you don't eat, Grablet." The many trees bore fruits of unusual shapes and sizes. Danni couldn't resist trying as many as possible. She tasted two mauve crescents, four olive-green spirals, and three lemon triangles. She ate so much her shorts felt too tight and she wanted to lie down and sleep. She carefully set the jar next to her sandals, put the Grablet on top, curled up on her right side and soon was sleeping as peacefully as Webbers.

Dreaming of a wonderful birthday party where she was dressed as Chief Angel and rode on a cloud, Danni was deaf to the Grablet's warning cry. She didn't stir when she was gently lifted and carried away.

In fact, Danni did not awaken until she was underground. And only then did she feel something rippling beneath her.

It was a very strange feeling.

She sat straight up and bumped her head. "Ouch!" It was wiser to lie down again. She was being carried down a long, narrow tunnel. But what was carrying her? Danni reached down and patted with one hand. Whatever it was felt warm and smooth as a dog's belly. Moaning softly, Danni tried to get off. Gently, but firmly, she was pushed back. "Who are you?" she cried. "Where are you taking me?"

Her only answer was a dry rustling, like the sound of autumn leaves in a light breeze. She was carried to a spacious, hollowed-out room. In the dim light which filtered through a small hole in the ceiling, she saw the shadowy outline of a chair big enough for an emperor. Underneath her, the forward rippling ceased and a sideways ripple began. It edged her closer and closer to the chair until she found herself tenderly deposited on its plush and roomy seat.

Danni blinked. "Could you bring a light please?" she called to the shadows in front of the chair. "I can't see very well." She heard the rustling noises, and from the other side of the room came a bright lamp, rippling towards her. The lamp was not being carried by a person — it seemed to come on its own, dipping and swaying in wavelike movements.

Now she could see, as the lamp cast a circle of light. *"Ooohhh!"*

Crowded about her were hundreds and hundreds of plump, pinkish-coloured grubs. They were about as tall as her knees and they nodded and swayed, nodded and swayed incessantly.

"Ah . . . um . . ." said Danni weakly.

Expectantly, the grubs craned forward. They rustled and waited.

Danni noticed they had no eyes, just slits. She couldn't think of a thing to say so she leaned back in the rich chair and examined as much of the room as she could see in the glow from the lamp. The walls were covered in finely woven silk tapestries in intricate designs and sumptuous colours. Her chair was upholstered in the same fine silks in a pattern of stars and planets and strange flying objects. Danni stroked the arm. "It's like a throne for a queen," she murmured.

The craning grubs at her feet bowed low and long.

"Is this a throne?" asked Danni.

The grubs bowed low again.

"Where is your queen?" asked Danni.

A third time, the grubs bowed.

A ridiculous thought came into Danni's head. She giggled and scratched her ear. "You can't mean me?"

But once again the grubs bowed low.

"You do mean me." She looked down at her old shorts and Webbers' darned sock. I don't look much like a queen, she thought. The Grablet would laugh at the mere idea. She stared at the grubs. "The Grablet's up there," she said, pointing at the ceiling. Then she remembered the grubs had no eyes. "Do you think I could go up and get the Grablet?"

The grubs swayed and rustled. They moved restlessly, to and fro.

"What about my sandals?" she asked, wigging her left leg. "My foot is cold."

Another wavelike ripple began, and soon a pair of dusky-rose silken slippers with golden tassles were laid at her feet. Regally, Danni thrust out her socked foot and the grubs tenderly encased it in a soft slipper. They did the same for her bare left foot. The slippers felt luxurious, as smooth as cream. Danni began to feel a little more like a queen.

She decided to try and behave like one, although she wasn't quite sure what queens did. She began by clapping her hands smartly. "Faithful subjects, I believe it is time for the royal banquet. I am feeling a queenly hunger." She sat back in her throne and waited to see what would happen. A few minutes later, six plates made of woven leaves were rippling towards her on the backs of the grubs. Each plate carried a fruit, like those she had seen above ground, and they were soon arranged in front of her.

The grubs showed no interest in eating, so Danni took it as a sign that queens must eat alone. She ate until juice ran down her chin and dripped on her shorts. Shorts are simply not fit for a queen, she thought, clapping her hands again. "Bring me royal clothing," she commanded, "and a basin of warm water to wash my royal face and hands."

The grubs bowed and rustled and some left the room.

While she waited for her wishes to be obeyed, Danni tapped her fingers on the arm of the throne, watching the rustling grubs and wondering why they had brought her here. "What are you waiting for me to say?" she asked. "You have such a waiting look."

Craning foward, the grubs nodded, swayed and rustled as they had been doing all the time.

Danni's basin of warm water was made of lashed reeds. Bobbing and dipping, it was borne to her feet. Behind it came a silken towel the colour of mandarins and a magnificent robe of midnight blue studded with golden stars and silver moons.

"Queens prefer to be alone while they wash and change," Danni reminded the grubs, and a moving pink carpet obediently left the room. Danni was left quite alone. She washed in the warm water and dried her face on the towel. Then she donned the wonderful robe. It was light as a cobweb but much too big for her. A gossamer train floated like a waterfall behind the pleated skirt and Danni had to hold bunches of material in her hands to keep from tripping. It made an elegant swishing sound as she strolled about examining the ancient, frayed tapestries.

The tapestries appeared to tell a story. Danni recognised many pictures of the grubs and the fruits of Sifania but the designs were so complicated she couldn't understand the story.

She stood under the hole in the ceiling which let in air from above, wishing Webbers and the Grablet could see her all dressed up in the midnight robe. "Hello? Hello?" she called up the hole. "Are you there? It's me, Danni."

She listened, but heard only the rustling of grubs. They had returned and were neatly arranged about her in a semicircle, eagerly craning forward and still with that waiting look.

"I would like to go outside," Danni told them, "and I'd like to go now!" She watched them closely.

All at the same time, the grubs shook themselves vigorously. The answer was no! The back of Danni's neck felt hot. She glared at the grubs. "I am your queen! And I *will* go outside if I want to!" She strode towards the tunnel.

Hundreds of plump grubs blocked her way. They milled about her, lifting her off her feet and carrying her back to the silken throne.

As soon as she was seated, Danni tried to get up again. "You can't keep me here for some reason I don't know about!" she shouted. "I wasn't meant to be a queen. I'm just a very ordinary Danni!"

The grubs surged forward, wiggling over Danni's lap, sitting on her hands, squatting on her feet. Danni tried to push them off, she tried to kick them off, she tried to butt them off with her head. But, swiftly and silently, threads of gossamer silk had been spun. The threads were wound about Danni's limbs a score of times, binding her as tightly to the throne as a bandage binds a splint.

13

AID FOR THE BLIND

Trapped in her bonds, Danni raged. "Untie me, you grubs!"

To her amazement, the grubs bowed respectfully. The ones sitting on her hands and feet immediately started nibbling through the silk threads with wee, ivory teeth.

Danni rubbed her wrists. "I'm very sorry grubs, but I don't know what you expect me to do. If you won't let me go outside, could you bring my friend, Webbers, down here? There's also the Grablet. It wouldn't be hard for you to carry the Grablet. They came to Sifania with me and both of them are very clever. Maybe *they* will know what you're waiting for."

Amongst the grubs there was much stirring and plenty of nodding.

Danni waited eagerly. After a short delay, a detachment of about fifty grubs left the room and disappeared up the tunnel.

"Thank goodness!" Danni sighed and sat back. She clapped her hands, having decided to give a few orders to keep the rest of the grubs busy. "I'll have a crown and a ring and . . . and . . ." remembering that her mother had said she'd never be allowed to have such a thing, "and a shiny black motorbike with a gold stripe!"

In a few minutes, bobbing up and down on the backs of the grubs, came a cushion of the same dusky rose as the slippers. On the cushion reposed a crown of gleaming gold with six slender points. Topping each point was a diamond the size of a walnut.

"Very nice." Danni put on the crown and paraded regally around the room. The crown was far too big—it rested on her ears.

Another cushion arrived. On this was a ring dripping with diamonds and sapphires and sparkling like a thousand fireflies in the lamplight.

Danni had just placed the ring on her middle finger when there was a swirling movement and an extra loud rustling at the entrance. A very surprised Webbers was carried in on the backs of the grubs, just as she had been carried herself. He held her sandals and the jar of purple water. "Good gracious, Danni, what are you doing dressed like that?" he asked.

Danni laughed. "Hi, Webbers! Can't you tell? I'm their queen and they do anything I command, except let me go outside. So I asked them to bring you down here. Where's the Grablet?"

Webbers stood, taking care not to squash any of the grubs with his webs, and took the Grablet from a pocket. "Once again, I didn't hear the Grablet call out," he admitted.

"Not exactly your fault," explained the Grablet. "A grub sat on me. I must say, Danni, you look rather different from the last time I saw you."

"This is my queen's robe and my queen's ring." Danni bounced merrily and the crown slipped askew to cover one eye.

The Grablet hooted.

Webbers looked closely at the grubs. "I had better introduce myself," he said. "Although I've been here before, I didn't realise Sifania was inhabited. My name is Kroninkliwzotl—or Webbers, if you prefer."

"And I am the mighty Grablet," bragged the Grablet.

The grubs nodded, swayed and waited.

"What do you think they're waiting for?" asked Danni. "Ever since they brought me down here I've had the feeling they expect me to do something, but I don't know what it is."

Webbers wandered about the room, carefully, to avoid the grubs. "I can't understand why I haven't seen them before," he said. "Perhaps it's because I only came here to rest on the other occasions."

"Yes," agreed Danni. "They can't see, and because you sleep above the ground they couldn't have bumped into you like they must have done with me."

"They certainly do look as if they're expecting something," said the Grablet.

Webbers studied the silk tapestries. He moved from one to the other with increasing interest. "Well! So that's it!" In his hand, the Grablet started cackling.

"What have you found out?" asked Danni.

"Something amusing," tittered the Grablet.

Webbers laughed. "It's a case of mistaken identity."

"What do you mean?"

"Come closer, Danni, and look at these designs. They tell a story."

"I thought they did! But I couldn't make out what it was."

"It seems they were woven a long, long time ago by grubs with failing sight," said Webbers. "Look! Here you can see grubs wearing spectacles." Danni peered closely at the faded tapestry. She could just make out a line of grubs and they were, indeed, wearing large, black-framed spectacles.

Webbers moved to another tapestry. "And now you can see that the grubs' sight has gone. See the sticks they're using? Further along, down here, their eyes are closing. You can just see slits where they once were." Now that Webbers was explaining it so clearly, Danni could understand the story. She became very interested in it.

"And," Webbers continued, "the story goes on that a person from an unknown and distant planet — see the planets woven here — will come and rule over them and restore to the grubs the precious sight they lost so long ago."

"Webbers!" Danni stood on tiptoe. "That looks like you!" She pointed to a particularly fine piece of weaving which showed a golden-haired young man wearing a black tube.

The Grablet chuckled. "That's Webbers all right!"

"Look! There are your webs!" cried Danni.

Webbers threw back his head and laughed merrily. "That's what I meant about mistaken identity. You can see over here that I'm wearing a crown. The same crown you have on your head right now."

"You mean I'm not their queen?" Danni was just a little disappointed. She stepped into her old towelling shorts and pulled the midnight robe over her head. "I guess you'd better have this, Webbers, and here's the ring and . . ."

"Pshaw!" interrupted the Grablet. "I bet the grubs don't mind who wears the robe, or the crown, or even the beautiful ring for that matter. They're only interested in getting back their sight. That's what they're waiting for!"

"That's it, Grablet! We must help them!" cried Danni. "Webbers, what about RESTORATIONS? Can you give them a rhyme?"

"I certainly can." Webbers searched his pockets for the little book. The grubs, listening intently, swayed, craned and rustled excitedly about their legs.

"I'm not your queen after all," explained Danni. "I wasn't in your story." The grubs nodded and swayed.

"I'm sorry I couldn't help, but Webbers can. He's the one you've been waiting for." She took off the crown and handed it to Webbers. "You'd better put this on while you're saying the rhyme. And the ring too."

"If it pleases you," said Webbers graciously. He looked

very handsome under the golden crown, which was a perfect fit.

"Very kingly," approved the Grablet. "Dignified too."

Webbers found the page in RESTORATIONS dealing with the return of sight. It was headed: "Sight—all-purpose". He read the instructions and told the grubs to go above ground and bring back three fallen branches from the trees. Then he asked Danni to pack the grubs into a tight zigzag.

Danni had finished doing this and the grubs were patiently waiting when the branches arrived. Webbers broke up the branches and arranged them into an arrow pointing at the zigzag of grubs. "Dim the lamp please Danni," he said, and sat behind the arrow, crossing his legs.

In the silence which followed, not even one grub swayed or nodded. Taking the Grablet, Danni tiptoed behind the grubs and squatted near the entrance. She listened as Webbers spoke the words.

> Watch, oh watch, you Angels of the Night,
> For your brothers who cannot see your glory,
> For You, we pray with all our might,
> Will raise their lids. Oh! Let them tell the story
> Of how You came with a burning light,
> In a rush of wings, so cold, so white,
> And gave them back the Gift of sight!

"Lovely verse," whispered the Grablet.

From the tunnel behind Danni came a strange and frightening noise, like the flapping of heavy draperies in an empty house. With the noise came a breath of air as cold as an Arctic winter. The noise grew. It passed over and around the waiting zigzag of grubs. The icy air ruffled Webbers' golden locks beneath the glittering crown.

Suddenly, the dim lamp flared into a blinding fireball. From the fireball, streaks of lightning hissed and sizzled like a nest of snakes.

Danni huddled into a ball, burying her face in her knees. The eerie flapping noise and the bone-chilling wind passed around her, then faded away up the tunnel like a strange winter being departing forever.

Danni uncurled and peeped through her fingers. All looked as peaceful as it had before Webbers began the rhyme. The room felt quite warm and the lamp was burning low.

The Grablet gave an extra-long whistle. "That was really something!"

For a few minutes, Webbers remained sitting next to the lamp, head bowed and eyes closed. The grubs neither moved nor made a noise. They could have been completely paralysed.

Click! Webbers snapped his fingers. He reached over and turned up the lamp. Only then did the grubs make small movements. They twisted, they shuddered, they rustled softly.

"Let's have a look at them," suggested the Grablet.

Danni felt stiff from her cramped position. Back bent, she peered at the nearest grub. "Yes!" she cried. "Yes! Yes! Yes! I can see their eyes! They're blue. Blue as forget-me-nots!"

The grubs were quivering like dollops of strawberry blancmange. They gathered around Danni and Webbers, pressing against their legs, blinking, nodding and rustling. The Grablet gurgled. Danni flung her arms around Webbers. "Isn't it wonderful?" she cried.

Webbers held up his hands for silence. "Listen carefully, grubs. All of you can see just a little and I know you must be very excited. However, the cure will not be complete for three more days. You must stay in a dim light and on no account must you go above ground until the fourth day. Do you understand?"

The grubs nodded and bowed with great solemnity.

"Good! We three are going now but, one day, as your

silk story tells, I will return and see how you are progressing." He took the crown from his head and the ring from his finger and laid them on their cushions.

Danni folded the midnight gown with the shining stars and gleaming moons and draped it on the arm of the magnificent chair. For a moment, she stroked the silken seat. "This was my throne for a while," she told the Grablet.

"Never mind, Danni. It would probably have been boring being a queen after a time. You would surely have missed my poems," said the Grablet.

"I suppose you're right." Danni kicked off the tasselled slippers and arranged them neatly under the chair. "And the grubs would have been terribly disappointed when I didn't do anything about their sight. Also," she giggled, "a queen covered in mould wouldn't have been very nice for them. Think of the smell!"

"A Mouldy Monarch?" said the Grablet. "Unthinkable!"

Danni put on her sandals. "Goodbye grubs," she called out. "I'm so glad Webbers helped you."

The grubs made a pathway of honour, bowing and making no attempt to stop their departure. Danni and Webbers left the underground room and climbed the tunnel, crouching on all fours.

Outside, in the fresh air once more, Webbers paused to comb his hair. Danni chattered about the grubs and what had happened in the room. She tossed the Grablet high as a cricket ball and made a spectacular one-hand catch. "We've got the cube, so what's the next verse, Grablet? Let's get going before the Flizzard turns up." And she hurled the Grablet into the air again.

"Whoa! Just a second. Whoops!" shrieked the Grablet. "Remember my dignity. Don't drop me! Whoops!"

"I'll remember your dignity if you remember the next verse," said Danni.

In a sing-song voice, the Grablet chanted:

Journey on to Doublesun,
And wait a night or two,
Until a pinch of moondust,
Has settled in the brew.

"That's no problem," said Webbers, patting his cheeks and peering into his little mirror. "Although I've not landed there before, I do know where Doublesun is. In fact, I have something to try out for NITT while we're there."

"What is it?"

"It's called the Comfy Coolah Cap and it should be tried out in a hot place. Dear, dear, I do *hate* wearing anything on my head. It upsets my hair so much," and he clicked his tongue with annoyance.

"Perhaps I could try it out instead?" suggested Danni. "I don't mind wearing hats."

"Certainly!" agreed Webbers promptly. He brought his NITT notes up to date and handed Danni another Mos tablet.

A little later, in the gloominess of space, Danni suddenly groaned. "I've just remembered. I didn't get the motorbike I ordered from the grubs. Fancy me forgetting that!"

"Phew!" was all Webbers said, but he said it softly and in between breaths, so only the Grablet heard him.

14

DOINGS
ON
DOUBLESUN

"Isn't this lovely?" said Danni when they had landed on Doublesun. "It's just as pretty as Sifania, but in a different way." She held the Grablet on her palm and turned slowly so it could see.

"Fair to middling," replied the Grablet.

"Well, it's much better than your place!" snorted Danni.

Twin suns shone down on a very attractive scene of rustic shacks nestling in banks of orange, white and turquoise daisies, with shady trees, mossy banks and a little brook shimmering in the distance.

Webbers yawned and checked that his hair was still there. He took out his notepad. "Let me see. The magenta-coloured Mos was all right, wasn't it? We have to stay here a couple of days until . . . er . . . what was it Grablet?"

" 'Until a pinch of moondust has settled in the brew'," quoted the Grablet.

"Well, it's daytime now," said Danni, "and rather hot. Imagine having two suns!"

"That reminds me," said Webbers. "The Comfy Coolah Cap. Would you like to try it now?" After several false alarms, finding a roll of sticky tape, a plastic fish and a tube of burnt sienna paint, he came across a crumpled object in one of his lower pockets.

"Funny looking cap," said Danni.

The Comfy Coolah Cap was made of fine mesh. It was round, to fit the top of the head, and hung down in a flap to cover the neck. Around the crown were six metal circles. "Those are solar discs," explained Webbers. "They attract power from the sun — or suns in the case of this planet — to charge tiny batteries throughout the mesh."

"What's this?" Danni pointed to a dial on one side of the cap.

"Temperature control, I'd say," said the Grablet. "The higher the number, the cooler the cap, eh Webbers?"

"Quite right."

"I'll try number six," said Danni. She dialled the last number and put on the cap.

"Ha!" laughed the Grablet. "What a sight you look!"

"I don't care. My head feels as cool as the sea."

"Glad to hear it." Webbers yawned again. "I'm going to rest now. Please don't wander off without me, and if you see anything that wants to carry off any one of us then yell as loud as you can!" Floating horizontally into his usual position, he was asleep in an instant.

"Hear that, Grablet?" Danni said. "We're not allowed to go exploring without Webbers."

"Then we can chat."

"What'll we chat about? Why don't you tell me about your homeland? Do you have any friends?"

"Not really," replied the Grablet. "I suppose anybody else might find it rather lonely, but for me it's a very special place."

"It's so cold there!" Danni shivered, remembering the wind.

"Bracing!" retorted the Grablet. "Very bracing!"

"The wind frightened me a bit."

"There are voices in the wind. They tell me things and I listen to them."

"What do they say?"

"I couldn't begin to explain to someone like you," snorted the Grablet.

"How did you first meet Webbers?"

"He made a visit to my place. I don't think he worked for NITT then. He belonged to URC."

"URC?"

"Yes. Universal Rock Collectors. He had to go to different planets collecting small samples of rock and take them back to Lex. Anyway, he landed and in the dim light . . . ahem . . ." The Grablet coughed. "Well, he mistook me for a rock. Of course, he realised his mistake right away when I spoke to him."

"Of course." Danni giggled.

"We got to talking and I was able to give him much assistance regarding the unusual rocks to be found on my home ground."

"I s . . . s . . . s . . . see," stammered Danni, through teeth which chattered like a sewing machine.

"Hang on!" said the Grablet. "Why are you shivering? Great gollops! There's an icicle forming on your nose!"

"I think I turned the Comfy Coolah Cap up too high. Better try number two." She pulled off the cap and adjusted the dial. "It really works. It's like putting your head in the freezer."

"Perhaps you'd like to sing one of your songs?" suggested the Grablet with great generosity. "It might help warm you up."

Before the Grablet could change its mind, Danni launched into an extremely sad song about her ducks. The Grablet quickly picked up the words and sang along too. They sang it again, but faster. And again, but louder. They woke up Webbers. "What a racket!" he complained.

"Sorry," said Danni. "Have you had enough sleep?"

"Not really." Webbers let his webs float to the ground. He stretched. "However, it will have to do. Let's have a look in those buildings and see if there are any people about."

"I'm looking forward to a drink from that stream," said Danni, whose throat was dry after all the singing. She frog-jumped over the grass on their way to the wooden shacks. There were five of them.

As they drew nearer, the Grablet cackled.

"What's so funny?" asked Danni.

"All is not as it seems," it replied mysteriously.

At the first shack, Webbers rapped on the plank door. It gave a hollow sound. Nobody appeared.

Danni walked around it. "Hey! It's only a front!" she called out. "There isn't any back and there aren't any sides!"

"Really?" Webbers laughed and fingered his smooth chin. "How odd!"

The Grablet chortled. "I told you all is not as it seems."

"How did you know?"

"I picked up the feeling. I felt the vibrations."

Danni tramped around the other shacks, nestled among bright flowers. "They're all the same," she told Webbers. "Just fronts."

Webbers rubbed a flower petal between his fingers. "These aren't real," he said. "They're made to look like flowers."

"Peculiar! Anyway, I'm off to get a drink," said Danni. She ran to the little brook, still shimmering under some trees. She went down on her knees and bent over with cupped hands. She soon discovered the stream wasn't real, either — just shiny material made to look like water. "Well, Grablet," she said crossly, "you're so clever, tell me where I can find a drink."

"I'm working on it. Just pick me up and turn me around slowly."

Danni did so, and the Grablet cried out: "Yes! Yes! Try under that big crooked tree to your right, girl."

"Come on Webbers," said Danni. "Let's see how good the vibrations are this time." She touched the tree and said disgustedly, "It's just another pretend thing! You're not so clever Grablet."

Webbers searched among the paper moss fronds at the base of the tree and found a green suede bag. "What's this? Seems the Grablet did sense something."

Danni took the bag, opened the drawstring and peered inside. She saw a red thermos and two hunks of bread. Inside the bread was a great wedge of hard cheese. "Enough for a picnic," she cooed. "Grablet, I take back everything I said."

"Why do I bother?" sniffed the Grablet. "Some thanks I get!"

Danni and Webbers sat under the branches of the fake tree while Danni polished off the cheese sandwich. The thermos contained hot, sweet tea and Danni soon disposed of that as well. She was neatly replacing the bag among the moss when the Grablet coughed.

"If anyone's interested, I hear somebody coming."

Danni couldn't hear a thing. Nor could Webbers, but he got up anyway. "I trust your hearing, Grablet," he said. "To be on the safe side, we'll hide and observe these people before we make contact. Come and climb the tree, Danni. The branches look strong enough to hold us."

Holding the Grablet, Danni followed Webbers up the artificial tree and hid in the paper foliage. Through brightly painted, paddle-shaped leaves, she saw a little speck coming from beyond the cleared patch where they had landed on Doublesun. The speck grew bigger. It turned out to be a group of people.

"They seem rather ordinary," said the Grablet loudly.

"Ssh!" hushed Danni.

As the people drew closer, Danni saw that they were chocolate-skinned, and some had hair black as crows and others were bald as sausages. They were all dressed differently, in clothes which varied from sweeping caftans to something like ballet tights, with lots of variations in between. Some of them carried heavy boxes and some dragged trailers on wheels.

One man was shorter than the rest. He wore enormous dark glasses and puffed a cigar as fat as a sea slug. The cigar stayed in the corner of his mouth as he bellowed out instructions.

Not far from the tree where they hid, the group halted. One of the women brought the short man a folding chair. He sat on this and pointed imperiously, shouting commands and puffing at his cigar.

"He must be king," whispered Danni.

The Grablet giggled.

"Ssh!"

Some of the company moved around the banks of flowers, looking as colourful as the blooms. Those who possessed hair combed and twirled it into exciting shapes, like eagles on the wing, or miniature ladders, or S-shaped cobras. Those who had no hair just chatted among themselves. The heavy boxes and the jumble of stuff on the trailers were unpacked and all sorts of interesting equipment was set up.

Danni squinted to see more clearly. A loudhailer was brought to the man in the chair. Now she could hear exactly what he was saying.

"Okay, okay, get into it now. Take your positions where we left off this morning. Come on! Come on! Not much time left!" he shouted.

Webbers nudged Danni. "Do you see?" he whispered. "They're making a film." Strewn around the boxes were reels, sound equipment and lengths of cable. Cameras hung on long poles. At last, Danni understood why the shacks only had fronts and why the flowers, the trees, the moss and the stream were artificial — they were all part of a movie set.

Suddenly, all the cameras swivelled in their direction.

"They've seen us!" hissed Danni.

"Ha, ha! We'll be movie stars," cackled the Grablet.

"Ssh!"

Both were wrong. A bald young man, slim as a reed, and a young woman, plump as a hippo, with hair teased into a figure eight, strolled towards their tree. They were followed by operators trailing equipment.

"All right, Henry and Lena," bellowed the man with the cigar. "Start from Scene Three. Come on! Come on!"

"That man who yells is the director," whispered Webbers.

Danni looked down and saw Henry and Lena standing directly beneath her. Leaning dangerously to one side, Henry tried to take Lena in his arms. After a lengthy pause, while he tottered drunkenly trying to keep his balance, he crooned, "My darling. My darling."

"Cor!" said the Grablet.

"Ssh! If you say anything else, you'll go in my pocket," Danni threatened in a murderous whisper.

"Cut!" yelled the director. "I told you last week I'd changed my mind about the 'darling'. This is an oldtime movie. Call Lena your pigeon, or something that sounds old."

Henry scratched his bald head on the spot where a paper butterfly perched precariously. Staggering, he took Lena in his arms once more. "My old pigeon. Oh, my very old pigeon," he crooned.

"Cut!" boomed the director. "Look Henry, *she's* not old, the *times* are. Do it again!"

Drooping like a wet bandage, Henry bravely gathered Lena in his arms a third time. "Oh, my sweet little pigeon," he said.

"Cut!" shouted the director. "Look, don't try to think for yourself any more Henry. Lena's a big girl. Anyone can see that. Cut out the 'little'."

Lena nestled into Henry's straining arms. This time, Henry got it right. "My pigeon, my pigeon," he droned and tottered. He waited, trembling with effort, but the director didn't interrupt. "Let us partake of refresherments, my pigeon. Let us partake, here in the woods where your wicked papa cannot follow." Lena smiled like a cave, revealing lots of gum. Her top teeth were missing.

"Cut!" bawled the director. "What are you trying to do? Why did you leave your teeth out for this scene?" He lurched out of the chair and pounded over to Lena, shaking his fist.

Lena looked vague. "I'm sorry, Mac," she said, "I only took them out for a few minutes to give my gums a rest. I must have lost them somewhere."

"Find them!" thundered Mac. He flopped against the tree, which shook violently. Just in time, Danni managed to avoid falling by grabbing Webbers with her free hand.

Under the furious eye of Mac, the group lazily searched through the grasses and back the way they had come. The teeth, only slightly soiled, were found under a display of turquoise flowers. Lena put them in, Mac waddled back to his chair, the cameras rolled again.

Flashing her teeth, Lena smashed the paper moss as flat as an ironing board as she settled herself beneath the tree. Henry joined her. He attempted to put an arm around her waist but it only reached halfway. Gazing into Lena's eyes, black as coal, Henry blindly extended his other arm. "I have bread and cheese, beloved," he said. His hand patted the moss. "I have bread and cheese," he repeated, patting again. He tore his gaze away from Lena and looked in surprise at his hand.

"Cut!" yelled Mac. "What is it now?"

"The bag isn't where it should be," complained Henry. "I thought I left it in exactly the right position this morning, so we wouldn't waste any time this afternoon." He stood up and found the green suede bag behind the tree. "I could have sworn . . ." mumbled Henry. He shrugged and signalled Mac that all was well. Seating himself next to Lena, he stared into her eyes again.

The cameras rolled. Henry drew the bag towards him, saying, "I have bread and cheese, my beloved, and refresherments for your parched throat." He put his hand in the bag, wiggled it around a few times and flashed a worried glance at Lena's mouth. "I have no bread and cheese, beloved," he said mournfully. "How about a drink?"

"Cut!" shrieked Mac. He sprang up, toppling his chair, and raged over to the tree. Henry drew down the corners of his mouth. He showed Mac the bag to prove there was only a thermos inside.

"All right! All right!" bawled Mac. "Who pinched the food? Come on, who did it?"

All in the company shook their heads. "Not me!"

Mac wrenched the lid from the red thermos and held it upside down. Not a drop of tea was left. There was a minute of deathly silence while Mac's face puffed up as round as a chocolate sponge. "Whoever did this will pay. My word they will," he growled in such a deadly voice that Danni's teeth tingled and her fingers turned numb.

The wretched Grablet chose that exact time to giggle again.

15

MAC AND HIS MOVIE

"Who laughed?" demanded Mac, spinning around and glaring at Lena and Henry. Both of them looked back as innocent as babes. Mac grabbed a handful of his spiky hair and pulled savagely. "You're all trying to ruin me!" he roared. "Spies, the lot of you!" His shoulders began to shake, the cigar drooped, he sobbed and tears squirted from behind his dark glasses.

Henry and Lena didn't care. They shrugged and casually strolled over to join the rest of the company, who had turned away from Mac and were amusing themselves with other things. Some played cards, some read magazines, others talked and laughed together. Nobody took any notice of Mac weeping under the tree.

But Mac's shuddering shoulders made Danni feel guilty. She noticed the cigar becoming quite sodden. "I'm sorry," she called, in a small, shaky voice. "I ate your cheese sandwich."

Mac stiffened. He pushed his dark glasses onto his forehead and looked into the tree. His tears vanished. "Get out of there!" he barked, spitting out the shredded cigar. "Come down at once! Who are you?"

Danni put the Grablet in her pocket and slid down the tree, followed by Webbers. They stood contritely in front of Mac, who slapped his hands on his wide hips. "Spies!

Spies from that devil Culdo!" he bellowed.

The rest of the company dropped whatever they were doing and gathered around.

"No!" protested Webbers. "We're not spies. We're just visitors from another place. We only arrived a short time ago. Danni was very hungry and thirsty and when we found the bag I'm afraid she couldn't resist eating and drinking. I'm willing to pay for what she had."

Mac narrowed his black eyes in deepest suspicion. "We'll see," he said, "just as soon as she takes off that white make-up."

"But this isn't make-up," said Danni, touching her skin.

Mac took no notice. He summoned a woman from the company, who hurried over with a rag and scrubbed at Danni's face.

"Not so hard!" Danni pulled away, her cheek burning from its scrubbing. The woman looked at Mac, who seemed surprised. He pointed at Webbers.

The woman reached up to Webbers' face, but he caught her hand. "Just a moment." Taking the rag from her, he wiped delicately at his cheeks himself.

The cast murmured.

Mac whistled. "Not make-up!" he said, shaking his head.

"We told you that!" snapped Danni.

The company crowded closer and touched Danni's face. They moved on to Webbers. "Keep away!" cried Webbers. "Mind my hair!"

Immediately Mac looked suspicious again. "A wig!" he bawled. "I'll bet it's a wig!"

Webbers turned as white as vanilla ice-cream.

"No," said Danni hurriedly, "it isn't a wig. Webbers just naturally has long, golden hair." To prove it, she reached up and gave his hair a gentle tug. After that, she fumbled under the Comfy Coolah Cap and pulled at her own short and shaggy locks, showing that they, too, were positively attached to her scalp.

"Chair!" Mac managed to mutter. His chair arrived and he collapsed into it. "Cigar!" A fresh, fat cigar was thrust in his mouth. For a few moments, he puffed reflectively. "Well, I guess you are visitors, after all, but even so . . ." He stopped, took a deep breath and bellowed, "WHAT ARE YOU DOING RUINING MY MOVIE?"

"We didn't mean to ruin it," said Danni. "And anyway, I don't think we did. It's already pretty hopeless."

"Hopeless?" spluttered Mac. "Hopeless?"

Taking out the Grablet, Danni toyed with it while she thought what to say. "There are so many things wrong. For a start, it's very boring, and why does Henry wear a long, striped bathing suit?"

Mac leaned forward. "Do you mean he should be wearing a plain one? I told that wardrobe mistress . . ."

"No," interrupted Danni. "Why does he have on a bathing suit at all? I understand that Henry and Lena are fleeing from her wicked father. They aren't by the sea. Why is he fleeing in a striped bathing suit?"

"Aha!" yelled Mac. "Because the movie is set in the olden times!"

"There's something about that thermos which seems out of place too," continued Danni, "especially if it's olden times."

"Look, I'm the one making the movie," growled Mac.

"How long have you been working on it?" asked the Grablet.

"About five years," answered Mac, looking at Danni. "And I haven't enough time to keep being delayed by you." He shouted at the company to get ready for filming again.

"Five years!" repeated the Grablet.

"And this is only Scene Three," said Danni.

"How many films have you made?" asked Webbers.

Mac stood up and puffed out his chest. "I finished one

before I started on this. That devil Culdo hasn't even finished his first film, a so-called 'mystery epic'. It makes me the number one producer–director in Doublesun." For the first time, he chuckled contentedly.

"How many years did you work on the first film?" asked the Grablet.

Mac stroked his bristly chin. "Let me see. *Return To The Desert* took me, altogether . . . um . . . twenty-four, no . . . twenty-five years." He waved wildly at the cameramen before turning to face Danni again. "It's been showing in the city every night since. You see, I specialise in romances."

"And you started this new film five years ago?" said Danni. "That means *Return To The Desert* has been showing every night for five years? I don't believe it. I bet nobody goes to see it any more."

"Of course they do. The place is packed," said Mac. "It's the only movie in Doublesun."

"How terribly boring," said Danni and the Grablet together.

"Strange voice you have — it keeps changing," Mac said, staring hard at Danni and still not noticing the Grablet. "And it's not boring. It's a stirring desert romance. I go every night myself."

The Grablet laughed. "I think we should see this film."

"You can be my guests tonight," offered Mac. "Now be quiet while I see to *this* movie."

Danni and Webbers sat on the grass and watched the rest of the day's filmmaking. There was delay after delay. Nothing seemed to go right and although Mac twice more burst into tears, nobody took any notice. Henry split his bathing suit trying to climb the tree and the heel of Lena's shoe fell off. Lena's wicked father chased them on a bicycle but he couldn't handle it properly and crashed into the tree. By the time the twin suns were setting, nothing had been accomplished.

The company packed up and prepared to return to the city.

"I can't wait to see *Return To The Desert*," said Danni as she watched the equipment being packed away, "but we mustn't forget about the pinch of moondust."

"It gets rather hard to remember your mould when we're having all these adventures," said the Grablet.

"The Moldy Flizzard won't find it hard to remember," warned Webbers, taking out the jar. He took off the lid and handed it to Danni.

"How do I grab some moondust?" she asked.

"I suggest you leave the jar out in the open and let the moon . . ."

"Moons," interrupted the Grablet. "See those two small ones rising?" Danni looked into the evening sky. The Grablet was right. Two modest moons, sailing out from behind a cloud, cast their light over the grass and gilded the false shacks. She carried the jar to the crooked tree and wedged it firmly in a fork. Please don't let anyone, or anything, knock it over, she prayed to herself.

"Come on!" called Mac. "Let's move!"

Even though his day must have been very frustrating, Mac seemed quite cheerful as they walked to the city. He talked proudly of the glorious future for his new film, which was called *Flight Into Romance*.

The Comfy Coolah Cap wasn't working now the suns had set, so Danni took it off. "Can I buy that hat from you?" asked Mac. "It would be great for one of my romantic scenes. It has such style!"

"It's not for sale," replied Danni. "I'm just testing it for NITT."

When they reached the city, the travellers saw that it was a well-planned, orderly place with rows of square buildings. The members of the company went their separate ways and Mac led his guests to a low white house in the city centre. He showed them into a big room where one entire wall was made of glass. Pressing up against the glass was a telescope pointing across the street to another home with a wall of glass. Mac waddled to the telescope and peered through it. "Nothing doing," he muttered.

Danni looked through the telescope. All she could see was a room identical to the one she was in. "Hey Mac," she called. "A man just came in."

Mac's left eye joined Danni's right at the telescope. "That's Culdo," he spat. Culdo looked through his own telescope. He poked out his tongue at Mac. Mac did the same to Culdo.

"I don't know why you're making faces at each other," said Danni. "At least, I can understand why he makes faces at you, but why do you do the same to him? You're ahead of him in making movies, aren't you?"

Mac turned away from his telescope with a worried frown. "That's true, but Culdo's been making two films at once. If they're both finished soon, I could be put out of business until *Flight Into Romance* is finished."

"I see. Well, we'll just have to think of something," said Danni. "But right now, it surely must be dinnertime?" And she smiled winningly at Mac.

"Of course!" He brightened up and waddled over to the wall, where he pressed a big button. A panel in the wall slid open. Behind it was a glass oven containing a mountain of baked dinner. When Mac opened the oven door, a delicious smell wafted out. Stomach rumbling, Danni helped Mac unload the food on a table.

"I hope there'll be enough," Mac said, dubiously eyeing a pile big enough to feed twenty people. "I wasn't expecting visitors."

"I'm the only one who eats," Danni told him. Mac looked relieved. He removed the cigar from his mouth and Danni tucked the Grablet away in her pocket. The two of them sat at the table and waded hungrily into the food.

Long after Danni had given up and was sitting back,

full to the brim, Mac was still shovelling steak and kidney pie, potatoes, peas and pumpkin down his throat. "There's still a corner left to fill," he said when all the hot food was finished. He got up and rolled over to another panel in the wall. Behind it was a glass refrigerator from which he took a crystal bowl. "Care for some mousse?" he asked.

Danni sighed. "Couldn't eat another thing."

Mac looked pleased and ate the whole bowl of pineapple mousse himself. Leaning back, he smacked his thick lips, replaced the cigar in his mouth and hummed contentedly.

While Danni and Mac were eating, Webbers had been scanning the opposite room through Mac's telescope. He had seen Culdo do almost the same things as Mac, except that during his meal Culdo had been interrupted by a visitor. The visitor handed him a note. Culdo read it and jumped around, thumbing his nose in the direction of Mac's room.

Full of energy, Mac got up from the table and bustled around corner of the room which was his kitchen. Rolling up the sleeves of his multi-coloured smock, he began to peel potatoes. "Must have some supper ready for after the show," he explained. He prepared a stew, then whipped up a fruit flummery. After distributing these items to the oven and the refrigerator, he said, "Okay, off to the movie house."

Danni yawned and leaned on Webbers' arm. A voice from her pocket said, "It's been ages since I was taken to a film."

Mac's cigar drooped and he gave Danni a strange look. "What have you got there?" he asked.

"Just the Grablet."

"Just the Grablet indeed!" said the pocket crossly.

"Now I understand." Mac beamed. "You're a ventriloquist."

The pocket sniffed. "No, she is not!"

"You're pretty good. I may be able to use you in my movie," chuckled Mac.

"Huh!" said the pocket.

It was just as Mac had said. The movie house was packed to capacity. People were even sitting on steps between the aisles. Full of importance, Mac strode in, nodding to either side and puffing his cigar. A few people shook his hand while the rest gazed at Webbers and Danni, nudging each other and smiling. Mac and his guests sat in a specially reserved row. The lights dimmed. Mournful music began and the crushed velvet curtain drew back.

Return To The Desert was printed on the screen in letters of fire. A list of credits followed, then the story began.

"Take me out! Take me out!" urged the Grablet.

"Sorry Grablet, I don't mean to keep forgetting you," whispered Danni.

On the screen, an extremely swarthy, one-armed man, wearing a sunhat hung with corks, trudged up a dirt road. The audience was absolutely rapt. They gasped as the one-armed man dramatically threw off a heavy fur cape and wiped his forehead with a frilly hot-water bottle cover.

The Grablet cackled.

"Ssshhh!" hushed the audience.

Stifling her laughter, Danni watched the film star prepare a meal over an open fire. He found it somewhat hard with only one arm, and used his shoulder and chin to hold a silver ladle in a cast-iron pot.

From the audience came sighs of wonder. Mac settled in his seat and smirked at the shadowy rows of people nearest him.

The man on the screen stirred his pot. Without warning, a woman in a blonde wig and bright blue satin dress stretched as tight as skin floated down from nowhere to sit by his fire. The hero seemed to think this quite natural, as did the audience, who murmured excitedly.

But Danni, the Grablet and Webbers couldn't stop laughing.

"*Sshhh!*" hushed the audience.

A confused series of shots followed: Danni saw plaster camels with chipped noses; half a dozen desert sheiks wearing carpets and gumboots; a stuffed parrot; and several fights mixed up with hugs and kisses under a fake desert moon with a rip in its middle.

Because Danni and Webbers both had the stitch and because the Grablet kept cackling so loudly, they were forced to leave before interval and wait near the candy bar for Mac.

The audience streamed from the theatre, wiping away tears of emotion. They were followed by Mac, who had his jaw stuck out like a bulldog. "Why did you leave before intermission?" he demanded.

"Webbers gets a bad back if he sits still for too long," mumbled Danni.

Webbers scowled at her. "Now Danni, that's not tr . . ."

But Mac nodded. "Okay, but I hope you'll both see the next half. It really knocks the audience out."

"I can't believe it," said Webbers, with a straight face.

The Grablet cackled again, so Danni put it in her pocket. Mac had time to swallow four icecreams, three extra large packets of crisps and a box of chocolate creams before the bell rang to signal end of interval.

Danni decided it was smarter to keep the Grablet in her pocket, even though it made angry buzzing noises and shouted threats during the second half. This part of the movie included some amazing scenes with a cross-eyed heroine, set amid an odd selection of food, notably baked bean milkshakes and sardine cream cakes. It brought many romantic sighs from the audience.

At the close of the movie, someone sprang up and shouted: "The greatest romantic drama Doublesun will ever know! Three cheers for the director!"

The cheering nearly lifted the roof. Mac beamed and puffed. "Happens every night," he chuckled proudly.

As they stood up to leave, there was a movement on stage. A man trotted from behind the crushed velvet curtain. He held a piece of paper.

Mac was puzzled. "What's this? What's the manager of the movie house doing on stage? This hasn't happened before — not in five years!"

The manager went directly to a microphone on stage. In a voice quavering with excitement, he told the audience he had some marvellous news.

"I think I know what it is," Webbers whispered in Danni's ear.

16

THREE
NEW
SCREENSTARS

"Tonight," said the manager, "I have been informed by Mr Culdo Grinzelkepper that he has completed his two amazing mystery films."

Cheers, louder than those they'd given Mac, came from the audience. Mac turned a sort of khaki colour. He tottered backwards and dropped like a sack of wheat. The cigar toppled from his frozen lips.

"There will be a change of programme here at the movie house," continued the manager.

"No! No!" Mac whispered.

"Tomorrow night, we will be screening Mr Grinzelkepper's *Search For The Missing Pork Chop*." More cheers, and the manager held up his hand. "That is not all! The following week, we shall be screening his second dramatic mystery-tragedy, *Who Stole My Banana Custard?*"

This last announcement brought ear-splitting whistles and thunderous claps. Danni fanned Mac's shocked face with her hands, while Webbers stamped on the smouldering cigar. Chattering at the tops of their voices, the audience thronged out. Not one took the slightest notice of Mac.

Danni and Webbers helped Mac to stand and he staggered from the empty movie house leaning on their arms. All the way back to his home, he walked in a daze.

They eased him into a comfortable chair. Danni went to the drink machine next to the oven panel and poured him a mug of hot milk.

Webbers walked to the telescope and scanned the opposite room. "Culdo's there," he said, "happy as a clown." Danni had a look. Culdo was celebrating with some friends. He was pointing gleefully at Mac's window and laughing, slapping his sides.

Webbers stroked his golden hair and asked Danni for the Grablet. "Well my friend, here's a problem for you. How do we help Mac?"

"I'm working on it," snapped the Grablet, "despite being unnecessarily confined to that pocket!"

Danni encouraged Mac to take a few sips of hot milk. His eyelids flickered when she mentioned food, so she pressed the button to slide the wall-panel away from the stove. She found a spoon and heaped a pottery platter with Mac's stew. "Try this," she said.

Mac couldn't resist the delicious aroma. "I might manage a teeny bite," he whispered. Grabbing the platter, he gobbled up the entire serving, becoming more and more vigorous as he ate. After a second platterful, he seemed almost revived. Danni lit another cigar for him and he sat a little straighter, folding his pudgy hands over his stomach while Danni ate a small supper herself.

"Well," muttered Mac, "I'm not ruined yet. There's still *Flight Into Romance*."

Danni pouted. "But how long will *that* take to be finished?"

Mac slumped again. "You're right. I'm ruined!"

"No, you're not! Webbers and the Grablet will think of something." Danni looked over at Webbers who was still deep in thought, cradling the Grablet.

"Uh uh," denied the Grablet. "I've tried and tried, but when you think of attempting to speed up the way they make movies here . . . well, it doesn't seem possible. Have you ever thought of doing anything else Mac?"

Mac eyed the Grablet with a shocked and pained expression. "MOVIES ARE MY LIFE!" he bawled. Then he threw back his head and boxed his own nose. "I must be losing my mind! What am I doing, talking to that . . . that . . . lump of something!!"

The Grablet snorted. Webbers and Danni didn't bother to respond; they were too busy thinking.

For a time, the only sounds in Mac's room were the shouts of merrymaking coming from Culdo's house. Then a smile spread over Webbers' face and he began his beautiful, musical chuckle. "It may work," he laughed, wiping his eyes. "This is my idea . . ."

"Better be good," interrupted the Grablet, annoyed that it hadn't thought of anything.

"We do a serious film. We three travellers, I mean."

"That's not much of an idea!" scoffed Mac. "It takes years and years to make a movie and all our works, even his—" he jabbed a thumb towards Culdo's house—"are serious."

Danni and Webbers both looked at their hands so Mac wouldn't see their smiles. The Grablet started to hoot, but made it into a kind of hiccup instead.

"If you just let me go ahead," said Webbers, "I think I can promise that our film would not only be finished in record time but would be something new and interesting for the people of Doublesun."

"We're going to make our very own movie!" cried Danni, capering around the room. "We'll be stars!"

But Mac didn't seem at all impressed. "I give up," he said, spreading out his hands as if surrendering to someone.

"Does that mean we can go ahead?" asked Webbers.

"Okay, okay. I've been washed down the drain anyway. I'm finished!"

"Right," said Webbers, "that's settled. We'll start early tomorrow morning, which means we all rest now." Without another word, he tossed the Grablet to Danni and floated to his horizontal position above the floor.

Mac stared and stared. He rubbed his eyes. "I don't believe it! No! No! I've already had too many shocks tonight." He covered his face with his hands, leaned back in his chair and his whole body started twitching.

In two minutes, Danni heard him snoring. She tiptoed over, removed the dark glasses which were still on his forehead, took the cigar from his lips and laid a teatowel over his knees to keep him warm. "Goodnight, Grablet," she said, turning out the lights and lying down on some cushions.

Next morning, everyone woke early. While Mac prepared breakfast, Webbers spoke firmly to Danni and the Grablet. "I don't want you two asking any questions just yet. It's a matter of getting this film done as quickly as possible. I think we can finish by this afternoon."

"Wow!" Danni gasped. "Hear that, Grablet?"

"Listen Danni," Webbers went on, "you will sing some of your own songs. The ones about lost lovers, why birds fly, falling autumn leaves. You know, the sadder the better."

It was much more than she had hoped for. Danni was too happy to speak.

"And you, Grablet," continued Webbers, "will recite mystical and classical poetry of the universe. The harder the poems are to understand the better."

"Yes indeed," responded the Grablet joyfully. "No-one can beat me at that. This movie sounds quite superior, Webbers. It sounds dignified and suitable for someone of my stature."

Webbers smiled. "As for me, I shall do monologues on the meaning of life and on the search for one's inner self."

Danni raised her eyesbrows. She wondered if the audience might find that somewhat boring, but she didn't say a word. She couldn't bear to have Webbers change his mind about her songs.

When Mac bustled to the table with breakfast, Webbers told him that the entire film, which was to be called *Eternal Truths*, would be made without help from anyone else. "I can operate both camera and sound equipment," he explained.

Mac's mouth dropped open. His eyes rolled up to the ceiling. "But you'll need a director!" he exclaimed.

"I shall do that myself," said Webbers. "Rest assured that *you* will have all the credit for this film."

"Yeah! But what sort of film? No director!" Mac muttered to his nine poached eggs.

"Just be patient, Mac. If you let me take complete charge, you'll have the film by the end of the day."

Mac jumped up, dropping his cutlery. "This is madness!" he yelled, mopping his brow with a piece of toast. "It can't be done!"

Danni pushed Mac into his chair. "Here, have a cigar," she said, and popped a new one in his mouth.

Mac gave up. He asked for his dark glasses and hid behind them with his mouth buttoned. It took a few minutes for him to revive enough to explain how to get to his studio and another few to remember where the key was.

As soon as Webbers had the key, they left Mac's house and stepped into the bright new morning. The twin suns were brilliant gold in a clear aqua sky.

Danni almost raced down the street, begging Webbers to hurry. "Come on, I want to get started on my movie career!"

The studio was only just around the corner from Mac's house. It was light and airy and packed with equipment. While Webbers set up the camera and other necessary items, Danni placed the Grablet on a shelf and sorted out some dramatic costumes from a box. She found a sombre opera cape of a wet-mud colour for Webbers and a slinky black dress with batwing sleeves which was suitable for her own sad songs and which went well with the Comfy Coolah Cap.

"What about me?" asked the Grablet. "If we are making a serious film, I demand to be suitably attired."

"All right!" Danni laughed. "How about this?" And she dropped a floppy straw hat with a long speckled feather right over the Grablet.

"Very funny!" said the Grablet. "Take it off, at once!"

Danni tossed the hat aside and busied herself with donning the slinky black dress.

"Miserable, selfish earth-girl!" grumbled the Grablet. "Only interested in outfitting yourself! Hang on! What's that poking out of the box?"

It was a gossamer scarf of a delightful watery blue-green, like a tropical sea. Danni pulled it out, wound it round the Grablet and tied it in a flowing bow.

"Lovely," sighed the Grablet. "That will do perfectly."

The filming went off very well, with no hitches at all. Webbers filmed Danni singing her songs and the Grablet reciting its poetry. And Danni, after some simple instructions, filmed Webbers reciting his monologues. All three were very satisfied with their performances. Secretly, Danni thought she had been the best. By the end of the afternoon, the film was finished except for the written credits, which Mac was to do.

Before returning to Mac's house, they took a walk through the fields to the artificial tree where Danni had left the jar with the three ingredients collected so far. Danni carefully removed the jar from the fork and peered inside. "Look!" she said. "There are a few specks of glittery stuff on top. It must be moondust!"

The Grablet hummed and hahed a bit. "Mm, it's safe to say that it is moondust. However, it's not enough to form a pinch, is it? Let's see, there are seven specks. I doubt that so few would constitute a pinch."

Danni replaced the open jar in the fork. "We'd better have another look tomorrow," she said. "The Cure Song said we should stay 'a day or two', didn't it?"

"Ahem! I hardly like to mention this, Danni, but have you got hairy legs?" enquired the Grablet politely.

"Of course not! Why?"

"Well, when you reached up for the jar . . . and then again, when you put it back, I thought . . ."

"Thought what?"

"Have a look," said the Grablet.

Danni looked at her left leg. She felt it. Smooth as a pancake. She looked at her right leg, in the striped sock. "There's nothing . . ." she began. Then she noticed something poking from the top of the sock. Was that *hair* sprouting on her leg? No . . . pooh . . . now she could smell it. "Mould!" she yelled. "Webbers, the mould has come right up my leg! What'll I do? What'll I do?"

"Calm down," said Webbers softly. "Just pull up the sock to cover it."

"But what happens when it grows past my knee?"

"We'll worry about that later. Let's try to remain calm. There's nothing we can do about your mould at present. We have to stay on Doublesun a little longer for the moondust." He patted Danni's shoulder. "I know it's difficult, but try to forget your problem for now. Think about the film we've just made."

Danni tried. She kept her mind on Mac and thought of how popular he'd be again when the audience were weeping over her songs and exclaiming over the Grablet's wonderful poetry and trying to understand Webbers' intelligent monologues. After all, what was the point of worrying? As Webbers had said, there was nothing else she could do at present.

She linked arms with Webbers and walked over the

fields, through the cool evening, singing one of her own songs. By the time they reached the city and Mac's house, Danni had pushed all thought of the mould right to the back of her mind. While she set the table for the evening meal, she heard Webbers speaking to Mac in a low voice. "I want you to view this film by yourself. You'll soon see why I think it will go down well with the people of Doublesun."

Danni spent a second night sleeping on Mac's cushions. In the morning she woke to find Mac gone, but by the time she had washed her face and hands and combed her hair, he had returned.

"I've arranged with the manager of the movie house to announce that the new movie will be shown this afternoon, before the evening screening of Culdo's production," he said. "Your movie had better be good! My reputation is on the line!" After eating a box of bran flakes, three steamed cod and seventeen hot waffles with syrup, he left for the studio to do the credits.

Danni, Webbers and the Grablet spent the morning exploring the city. When they returned to the house, they were greeted by Mac who swooped on Danni. "Great, great movie!" he trumpeted, shaking her so hard she bit her tongue.

"You must really appreciate the finer things of life," said the Grablet in a surprised voice.

"Like my songs, for instance?" said Danni when she got her breath back.

Mac threw back his head and roared with glee. "I appreciate every part of it! Every single part of it!"

"I trust you finished the credits?" asked Webbers.

"Yes I did," replied Mac, beaming like a radiator. "Oh boy! This movie is a first for Doublesun, all right!"

17

ASTONISHING AFTERNOON

Danni skipped all the way to the movie house, almost leaping out of her skin at the thought of seeing herself on the screen. Long queues of people waited outside. Above the entrance was a mighty poster in letters of luminous green.

Eternal Truths
An Entirely New Type of Film. A Comedy.
Produced by Mr Mackenzie Murgatroyd
and Starring Webbers from Lex
and Danni from Earth.
Also, at GREAT EXPENSE,
from Far-Flung Corners,
the Astonishing Grablet!

Danni frowned. "Why have they put 'comedy'?" she wondered aloud.

"Mac's got it wrong in his excitement," said the Grablet. "Isn't that right Mac?"

But Mac was busily shaking a forest of hands and didn't hear.

"That must be it," said Danni. She soon forgot the error because she suddenly noticed that quite a few moviegoers were wearing headgear. "Comfy Coolah Caps!" she cried.

Mac turned from the hands for a moment. "Ha ha. I

got my publicity section to run up a whole pile of those caps to be handed out to the audience at the premiere. I've really stolen a march on that devil Culdo. First, a surprise movie and second, a new cap to go with it!" He bustled ahead, pumping more hands.

"But Webbers," whispered Danni, "those Comfy Coolah Caps don't seem quite the same as mine. The solar discs look like bottle tops!"

Webbers laughed. "That's what they are — ordinary bottle tops. And the mesh is ordinary chicken wire. Mac asked about the Comfy Coolah Cap again and I tried to explain its real purpose but he wasn't in the least bit interested. He was more concerned with the fashion than the special reason for the cap. The people of Doublesun have really taken to it."

Danni had to agree. Those who were lucky enough to have caps were preening and strutting like proud pigeons.

When the doors opened and every single seat was taken, Mac did some strutting of his own, in front of the audience. He made Danni and Webbers strut with him. On all sides, they were hailed with cheers and applause.

"Thank you, fans. Thank you, thank you," carolled the Grablet.

It took quite a lot of shushing and hushing before everyone was quiet but, at last, the curtain drew back and the movie began. One of Danni's scenes was shown first. It featured a most melancholy song about a young girl begging to die because she'd lost her boyfriend. Danni thought she looked suitably pale and interesting in the long black dress and she was greatly pleased by the quality of the sound. Every word of her heartrending song was as clear as a bell. Breathlessly, she waited to hear the first sniffle from the audience.

Instead, a titter rippled through the front row of the movie house. It was taken up by the second and third rows, and then the fourth, and so on, until the entire audience was giggling. Then the giggles grew into loutish guffaws.

"QUIET!" commanded Danni. "You'll miss some of the words!" But the audience went on laughing. Danni's song was completely drowned out.

The Grablet appeared next. "Now they'll hear something to make them think," it purred. However, after the first few lines of the Grablet's sensitive poetry, the audience was laughing uproariously, whooping and gasping for breath.

"What's going on?" demanded the Grablet.

"Search me!" Danni said crossly.

When Webbers appeared on the screen and spoke his thoughtful monologue, the audience began rolling in the aisles, clutching their sides. On and on went the whoops, the gasps and the laughter, increasing with each new song, poem and monologue.

Danni and the Grablet got crosser and crosser, but Webbers only smiled serenely.

Mac was overcome. Tears of laughter soaked his scarf. He had a stitch in his side. At the completion of *Eternal Truths*, he moistly embraced Webbers and Danni and even congratulated the Grablet.

"Are you kidding?" responded the Grablet, sounding very injured indeed.

"Nobody has seen anything like it before!" whooped Mac. "It's the success of the age!"

Even Culdo, who had come to watch the movie out of curiosity, pumped Mac's hand. "I have to hand it to you, Murgatroyd," he said. "Comedy is the thing, and you gave it to them today. I didn't even know you were making this movie, you crafty old fox!" They went off together, arm in arm, swept away by the delighted crowd.

Danni stood glaring at Webbers.

Webbers tried to wipe the smile from his face and explain what had happened. "Don't be angry Danni, nor you, Grablet . . ." he began.

"But I am!" growled the Grablet. "I don't think I have

EVER been so angry!"

"Listen," said Webbers. "I worked out that if the people of Doublesun thought Mac's romances were serious then they were sure to think that a serious film was funny. After all, people do look at things in different ways, don't they?"

Danni and the Grablet took a short time to understand but a longer time to calm down. Eventually, Danni sighed. "It's not nice to have people laugh at my sad songs," she said, "but I can see what you mean Webbers."

"Humph!" snorted the Grablet.

"Anyway, we have to get on with collecting things for the Cure," said Danni. "We can't stay on Doublesun and be movie stars forever."

"Quite," agreed the Grablet. "The sooner we go the better, as far as I'm concerned."

Mac was heartbroken when he learned they were leaving. "But you are my true friends," he sobbed. "You can't go now!"

He cheered up when Danni gave him half an apple pie she found in the refrigerator. "I hope you and Culdo won't make faces at each other any more," she said.

Mac beamed at her. "No, no. We've decided to dismantle our telescopes. We're no longer going to spy on each other and, on Double-Sundays, we're going to invite each other for tea. After all, we're equal in the movie race, thanks to you. Thanks to *all* of you, my dearest friends!"

Danni handed him the original Comfy Coolah Cap. "Webbers said I could leave this with you. If you wear it and twiddle the dial, you can keep your head cool while you're making movies."

Mac whooped and gave her a bear hug. "I'll put it in a glass case!"

"But you're supposed to wear . . ." began Danni.

He wasn't listening. "I'll have thousands of coloured lights winking around it. People will come to see it, the first, the original Comfy Coolah. It will be a kind of shrine.

It will forever remind me of you." And he burst into tears.

"What's wrong?" asked the Grablet.

"I love you all! You grab me here," and Mac clutched at his heart just as his entire wall of glass smashed inwards in a monstrous explosion. For a moment, Danni thought Doublesun had blown up. Glass flew around like hailstones. The floor quaked. The walls seemed to lean crazily.

But it wasn't the end of Doublesun, after all. The glass stopped flying, the floor felt steady as a rock, and the walls stood as straight as ever. There was only a hole where the glass wall had been and a ringing in Danni's ears.

There was a second of stunned silence, then a long snout on the end of a slithery neck poked through the hole and began snuffling over Mac's shoulder.

"S . . . some trick of Culdo's?" stuttered Mac.

"Not Culdo!" bellowed Danni. "It's the Moldy Flizzard! It's caught up with me!" Webbers was already taking a deep breath. Danni needed no urging to grab hold of his shoulder loops. She had them firmly in her grip before Webbers finished a second breath.

"Don't forget me!" came a shout from the floor. Danni couldn't remember having dropped the Grablet. She had to waste a precious second and pick it up.

Rapturously, the Moldy Flizzard sniffed at her legs. "Mimi," it trilled, "mimi mi mi mimi."

"Mimi?" repeated Mac. He looked as if he'd received a clout to the head and was still in shock.

"Gotta go!" cried Danni as Webbers sailed up to the ceiling. They flew over the craning neck of the Flizzard and out through the hole, leaving the monster sniffing at air.

"It doesn't seem fair," Danni said as they left the city.

"What doesn't?" asked Webbers.

"Leaving Mac alone with the Moldy Flizzard."

"Let's worry about Mac after we've collected your jar.

I hope it's there!"

The jar was still safely wedged upright in the fork of the fake tree. A few more specks of glittery stuff floated on top of the liquid.

"That'll do," said the Grablet. "We can't hang around here any longer."

Webbers screwed the lid on tightly and stowed the jar in a top pocket. "Tell me the next verse," he said.

"This is it:

> *Just one more special item,*
> *You must pop into the drop,*
> *You'll find it out on Zubel,*
> *For that's your final stop."*

"Last stop, hooray!" shouted Danni. "I'll soon get rid of this mouldy leg. Wait a minute! Zubel, did you say? Flizzards come from Zubel . . .!"

"Can't be helped," said Webbers. "We're off to Zubel. At least I know the place. Ready, Danni?"

"Yes, but . . ." Danni scuffed her sandal in the paper moss, "well . . . what about Mac? His whole wall was smashed in. We can't just leave him all alone to cope with the Moldy Flizzard."

"We'll take a quick look," said Webbers, "to see if he's hurt. We can't do anything about his wall, I'm afraid."

"This is madness!" shrieked the Grablet. "We should be nicking off imediately!" Despite the Grablet's protests, Webbers flew back to the city with Danni hanging on behind.

Danni's mind had imagined all sorts of terrible things going on at Mac's house. But what she saw was a complete surprise.

Far from menacing Mac, the Moldy Flizzard was stretched out cold. It lay half in and half out of Mac's house. On its huge belly danced Mac and Culdo, hand in hand.

Mac's mouth was frothing at the corners. "Look what we've got!" he cried.

Webbers was aghast. "How did you do that?" He stared at the lifeless Flizzard. "You haven't killed her, have you?"

"No, no! Mimi's not dead. Culdo heard the glass smashing and came over to help."

"But how did you knock her out?" asked Danni.

"With this —" Culdo brandished a long-needled syringe. "I use these things in my amazing mystery movies. I just went *sprong* into Mimi's knee — the part of her closest to my eye. Down she came. Easiest thing I ever did!"

"You picked the right spot," said Webbers.

"Culdo and I have our next movie in the bag!" yelled Mac, gambolling like a lamb. "It will be a joint production by Murgatroyd and Grinzelkepper."

"Grinzelkepper and Murgatroyd," corrected Culdo.

"Okay. If you insist," grinned Mac. "Anyway, it's a giant mystery-romance called *Who Does Mimi Love?*"

"A romantic Flizzard?" scoffed the Grablet.

"We start filming tomorrow," said Mac. "After we've finished *Who Does Mimi Love?* we'll make *Mimi on Roller Skates* and, after that, *Mimi Solves a Mystery* and . . ."

"You will be careful, won't you?" interrupted Webbers. "Moldy Flizzards are very strong and powerful. You'll find that out when she wakes up!"

"Don't worry about us!" flapped Mac. "We've got Mimi under control, haven't we Culdo?"

Culdo chuckled. "Our next movie is as good as made. All we need is a romantic rival to play opposite Mimi and her boyfriend." He glanced at Danni. "You weren't bad in the comedy. Are you interested in another part?"

"Not in the least, thank you," babbled Danni. "We're going now." She waved to Mac. "Goodbye again. Good luck with your next movies."

Reluctantly, Mac and Culdo came outside to see them

off. Both were anxious to get on with discussing their plans. "See ya, then," said Mac, waving before Danni had even swallowed her Mos tablet.

"So that was Doublesun," she remarked as they rose into the air. "Some of my best work lies back there and people will be laughing at it every afternoon."

"At least the Flizzard is lying there too," said the Grablet. "I hope Mac and Culdo keep it under control long enough for us to reach Zubel and collect the final ingredient for your cure."

18

IN
A ZUBEL
SWAMP

The Grablet insisted on reciting endless poems during the journey to Zubel. Fed up with listening, Danni started singing to drown out the Grablet. Their combined voices made Webbers fly much faster than usual.

When Danni was hoarse from singing and wondering whether she could keep it up any longer, Webbers passed her a blue Mos. "Nearly there?" she croaked.

"Straight ahead," said Webbers.

Zubel was a medium-sized planet of murky ochre colour, draped in a covering of heavy clouds. Webbers descended so rapidly that Danni stiffened herself for the bone-shattering bump which must surely come. The yellow-brown land zipped up to meet them. She gritted her teeth.

But there was no bump, no shattering jar of bones. A pair of large webs and a pair of small feet dived slap bang, into a Zubel swamp!

"Pooh!" cried Danni.

"Mm," Webbers grunted. "Made a mistake. Thought it was land. At least it's not too deep here."

"Foof! I can't see the bottom," complained Danni, who was up to her waist.

"Don't let *me* fall in!" shouted the Grablet. "There are

Flizzards here and I hate swamps. Get on dry land, quickly!"

"Everything looks the same," said Danni. "Which way do I go?"

"Aim for that tall tree over there," said Webbers.

Danni waded towards the tree, her feet sinking into the oily bed of the swamp, stirring up swirling clouds of sediment. The tree was covered with masses of sweet-smelling pale-pink blooms. Using an overhanging branch, Danni hoisted herself out of the swamp. She stamped her feet. It did seem firmer underfoot, but very muddy.

She gave a helping hand to Webbers. "I wonder if it's mud that we have to collect here," she said. "If so, there's plenty to choose from. What's the last thing for the jar, Grab . . . oooops!" She lost her footing and slid backwards down a mudslide.

Webbers caught her around the waist just in time to save her from another dip in the swamp, but then his webs slipped. Both of them skidded over the slick yellow mud, trying to stay upright.

"It's firmer over here," puffed Webbers, attempting to swing Danni nearer the tree.

Snap! Zing! Something rushed past Danni's nose. Her breath was sucked from her lungs, her ankles pincered, her head briefly scooped the mud. In a moment, her whole world was upside down — the sky above her feet, her head dangling above ground.

The zip on her pocket gave way. The Grablet slid out — *plop!* It was half-swallowed in mud.

"Webbers! Webbers! I'm . . . I don't know . . . what's . . .?"

"Look to your right," said a familiar voice.

Danni did. Webbers hung upside down just as she did, both of them caught around the ankles by a rope.

"Look what you've done!" the Grablet roared. "You've let me get all dirty down here!"

"Never mind about you," replied Danni. "What about us? You don't think it's nice being up here, do you?" Her cheeks were as rosy as raspberries. "Can you get us down Webbers?"

"There's a knife in one of my pockets. If I can get to it, I might be able to swing up and cut my ankles free."

"Well, get on with it!" urged the Grablet. "Come and rescue me!"

It was easy enough for Webbers to lift his arms and unfasten a pocket but, as soon as he did, everything in the pocket fell out. *Splat! Clop! Slap!* A measuring tape, a pair of scissors and his notepad tumbled out, followed a second later by his blue folding umbrella, which clipped the Grablet.

"Trying to finish me off, I suppose?" snarled the Grablet.

"Sorry," said Webbers, opening another pocket. "I'll be more careful this time." Despite his care, the contents of the second pocket also slipped out before he could grab them. RESTORATIONS, a metal caterpillar, a piece of lemon soap, a teaspoon and five sticks of tobacco joined the rest of the things in the mud.

"Don't try again," warned Danni. "What if the jar falls out?"

"That's in my top pocket," said Webbers, "and I won't touch that one." He was about to unfasten another pocket when the Grablet gave a low whistle.

"Psst! Can you hear it?"

There was a faint slurp, slurp of water.

"Probably a Flizzard coming up the swamp," said Webbers.

"HELP!" yelled the Grablet.

"You know as well as I do that Flizzards won't bother you unless you've touched their egg," said Webbers.

"But what if it's Danni's Flizzard?" roared the Grablet. "It could tread on me! I'd be lost forever in this rotten, stinking mud!"

"You always think about yourself, don't you?" snapped Danni. "You're not bothered about us hanging upside down, are you?"

"Well, what can I do about you anyway?"

Danni couldn't think of anything. The slurp of water was louder. What if it *was* her Moldy Flizzard? Just when she'd been so close to getting the last thing for the Cure.

"It's not a Flizzard," said Webbers. He hung lower than Danni and had a better view through the pink flowers to the swamp. "It's a boat! HERE!" he shouted. "OVER HERE!"

Danni heard two voices. A male voice and a female one. Then she heard a hollow thump and a scrape, and the sounds of feet squelching through the mud.

"Look at that, Fly!" squeaked the female voice.

Directly beneath Danni was a thin, upturned face, with hazel eyes and a blobby nose, surrounded by copper curls. The woman wore dungarees the colour of Zubel mud.

"It's people, Gwenda," said the male voice.

Danni saw another upturned face. A nose with a high bridge, no eyebrows whatsoever, and moustache and hair like silver. He also wore dungarees.

"They're not like us, Fly!"

"Anyone can see that, Gwenda."

"What do you think they're doing here, Fly?"

Webbers swung on the rope. "We're visitors," he said. "Can you help us down please?"

"Did you set this trap?" asked Danni. "You should try it some time, it's horrible!"

"They could be dangerous, Fly," said Gwenda.

"We are not!" yelled Danni.

Fly moved closer, reaching out his hand to touch Webbers' hair.

"GET OFF ME!" shrieked a furious voice.

Fly jumped. He grabbed Gwenda. Gwenda slipped. Fly somersaulted over Gwenda and both landed on their bottoms in the mud. "Something talked!" jabbered Fly. "It was under my foot. A talking stone!"

"Stones don't talk," said Gwenda.

"*Buzz, buzz, buzz!*"

Fly leapt up. "There!" he said. "Didn't you hear it?" He sluiced around in the mud with his fingers and brought out the Grablet.

"FOOL!" roared the Grablet. "First you tread on me and then you SIT on me, you IDIOT!"

"Go on Grablet," urged Webbers. "Tell them who we are. We want to come down."

"Look Fly, look!" Gwenda pointed excitedly. "There are lots of things here. That talking stone isn't the only thing!"

"I AM NOT A TALKING STONE!" yelled the Grablet.

"Flingo!" yelped Fly. He picked up the tobacco. "I haven't seen anything like this since Simba." He smelled it. "It's real snifter!"

"Here's a book," said Gwenda wonderingly. She snatched up RESTORATIONS and wiped the mud from its cover. "Can you still read, Fly?"

"Listen!" called Webbers. "Before you do anything else, could you help us down . . . *please!*"

Fly and Gwenda took no notice. They kept their heads together, absorbed by RESTORATIONS, turning over the pages and exclaiming at the rhymes.

"Can't you hear, idiot?" said the Grablet. "First let Webbers and Danni down, then you can read that book."

"Quiet, stone!" ordered Fly. "Look, Gwenda, these poems are all about parts of the body. I like poems. Remember all those poems I used to write when we lived on Simba?"

"Don't say any of them!" cried Danni. "It's dangerous!"

She might as well have talked to the mud. Fly continued to turn over pages, his nose twitching with excitement. "Gwenda! If you can believe what this book says, then you can get back anything you've lost."

"What do you mean, Fly?"

"Just what I said, Gwenda!"

"Please don't say any of those rhymes," warned Webbers. "Only I am permitted to say them."

Gwenda sneered at Webbers. "Oh, you'd tell us anything. You just want to come down."

"Read the back page," Danni pleaded. "Please read the back page first."

But Fly hollered unheedingly. "Gwenda! Here's a poem about eyebrows! Eyebrows, Gwenda! Get some flowers!"

"Flowers?"

"Reach up and get some flowers," commanded Fly. "It says here, I have to hold some flowers while I say the poem."

Gwenda looked bewildered, but she hurriedly plucked a bunch of the pink flowers and gave it to Fly.

"I'm not joking," pleaded Webbers. "Something nasty will happen to you if you don't let *me* say that rhyme!"

"Rubbish!" snorted Fly. "Okay Gwenda, you hold this stone and . . ."

"I AM NOT A STONE!" bellowed the Grablet.

" . . . and I'll sit here holding the flowers," continued Fly, as if he hadn't heard. He cleared his throat and smiled up at Gwenda. "Soon I'll be as handsome as I was when we first met, Gwenda — before my eyebrows were shaved off by that saucer you threw at me."

"For the last time!" ordered Webbers. "Will you listen to me?"

"No!" replied Fly. "Just keep quiet or you'll stay there for good!"

"Serves you right if you get the works," said the Grablet nastily. "And I hope you do! Stone, indeed!"

Danni and Webbers were forced to hang helplessly from the tree while Fly said the rhyme:

> *Green Princess of the Shades,*
> *Leave your Shadows,*
> *Leave your Glades.*

I call you now unto this place,
I call you from your emerald fields,
Lift gentle fingers to this face,
Create once more the missing shields.

"That's it!" Fly closed RESTORATIONS with a snap and waited confidently.

Webbers, Danni and the Grablet also waited, but not so confidently.

Gwenda tittered nervously.

Nothing happened. Fly lost his confident look and frowned. He called out, "Where are you, Green Princess?"

From out of nowhere, a bell tinkled. Fly half-rose from the mud. The bell tinkled again. "Something's happening," muttered Fly.

Something did. Suddenly his head was snapped back and his cheeks, nose and ears were massaged violently by unseen hands.

"Knock it off!" mumbled Fly. "It's the eyebrows, remember? Just get on with the good work, Princess, and make it snappy."

A gasp of fury from an unknown voice resounded over the swamp. Fly's head was immediately tossed from side to side like a punching bag.

"Stop! Stop!" yelped Fly. "No more! I'm sorry!"

The pummelling ceased, but that wasn't the end of Fly's punishment.

"*Yeowch!* My nose!" Fly started slapping at air in front of his face.

Hardly believing her own eyes, Danni watched as Fly's nose began to grow and grow. It snaked out longer and longer, until its weight made it droop to the mud, where it still continued growing, like an endless finger.

Fly bayed like a wolf in the wilderness. "*Yaroo, yaroo, yaroooooooooo!*"

Frozen on her feet, Gwenda clutched the Grablet and stared in horror as Fly's amazing nose lifted up by itself and rapidly twisted and turned, twisted and turned until it had formed a neat plait. At the end of the plait, the nostrils pointed up to the sky.

The bell tinkled again and, quite clearly, everyone heard the sound of hands being dusted off. Then there was silence.

Nobody moved a muscle for at least five minutes.

Gwenda was first to break the silence. "Oh Fly," she moaned.

"We warned you!" said Danni.

Fly flopped stiffly onto his back, holding the flowers above his chest like a funeral posy.

"He's in shock," said the Grablet. "Knocked flat!"

"Now will you let us down, Gwenda?" asked Danni. "We told the truth."

Gwenda was still rooted to the spot.

"GWENDA!" shouted the Grablet. "Get a hold of yourself, girl. Let my friends down, at once!" Like a robot obeying its master, Gwenda stalked to the boat and returned with a knife. Still in a daze, she wandered behind the tree.

Danni heard the chop of metal through rope. Slowly, she dropped closer to the ground as the rope around the branch grew longer. She swung herself to the side to avoid landing on her head.

Webbers was already standing up, shaking mud from his hair.

Gwenda bent to cut the rope from their ankles. "This must have been an old, leftover trap," she murmured, holding one hand over her nose. "Fly and I haven't made any since the others left."

"What others?" asked Webbers.

"All the others. They've gone." Gwenda straightened up and stepped back a few paces, squeezing her nostrils together. "They all left," she mumbled through her nose. "They didn't like all the swamps and the Flizzards. Too much work to drain the land. What are you going to do about Fly?"

"There's nothing I can do," replied Webbers. "He shouldn't have read that rhyme."

"He's a moron!" sniffed the Grablet.

"He'll have to learn to breathe through his mouth," said Danni.

Gwenda stepped back further. She looked green. "How long are you staying?" she asked.

"Not long," said Webbers, picking up the things which had fallen out of his pockets. RESTORATIONS was the first to be buttoned away securely. "We only have to get one thing from Zubel."

Gwenda started to heave.

"Are you sick?" inquired Danni. "You've gone a funny colour." She reached over to pat Gwenda. "You mustn't worry about Fly, he'll be . . ."

"Keep away, *eeeooorrrk* . . ." groaned Gwenda.

"But . . .?"

"Look Danni," said the Grablet, "there's no kind way to say this. You stink! In fact, you stink to high heaven!"

"I suppose I do!" snapped Danni. "Webbers and I landed in that dirty swamp, you know!"

Webbers put his arm about her and said gently, "It's not just that, Danni. The sock isn't doing its job any more."

So much had happened that Danni hadn't given much thought to her mould since they had landed on Zubel. She looked. The sock was a mass of holes. Strand after strand gave way, the wool disintegrating in front of her eyes.

"Looks like the swamp finally rotted it," said the Grablet.

As the last strands parted, Danni's mould was totally exposed, glistening and treacly and blooming with fully open fungus flowers.

It had grown way up past her knee to the leg of her shorts.

19

DANNI'S DECISION

"What an awful sight!" wailed Danni.

"You look like a Flizzard's egg," said Fly. He was on his feet at last, his plaited nose standing out half a metre from his face.

Gwenda was choking. "She smells as bad as that orphaned egg we left up the bank, doesn't she Fly?"

"Can't smell a thing," said Fly cheerfully.

"Your poor, poor nose," sighed Gwenda.

"Serves me right." Fly snapped his fingers at Danni and Webbers. "I should have listened to these people, but I was too stupid."

"Yeah!" agreed the Grablet.

"Looks like you were stupid, too," Fly said to Danni. "You must have touched a Flizzard's egg."

Danni admitted that she had. "I kicked an egg and broke it, but we've been collecting things to cure me of the mould."

"I didn't know there was a cure. Gwenda and I stayed behind on Zubel because we like to help Flizzards, but we've never *ever* touched an egg."

"Best if you never do," said Webbers, combing his hair. "It takes a lot of travelling to find the Cure ingredients."

"Just one last thing to get," said the Grablet, "then we can be off . . . oh joy! Home again!"

"Well, what is it?" demanded Danni. "If I stand here much longer the mould will reach my head."

The Grablet yawned. At least, a few holes opened wide and it gave a sound like a yawn. "Da da, de da, da da da . . . out on Zubel, for that's your final stop."

"We know that!"

"Um . . . add the pink . . . ah, yes!

Add the pink rose of the swamps,
With the stem of green quite hollow . . ."

"And?" said Danni. "What's next?"

"Ah . . . yawn . . .

Now the brew has all it needs,
Gulp it down in one big swallow."

"The pink rose of the swamps," said Danni. "Where can I find that, Fly? Gwenda?"

"Right here," said Fly, flourishing the bunch of flowers he still clutched. "This is the pink rose of Zubel. I say," he looked admiringly at the Grablet, "I did like that poem you just said. I'm a poet too, you know."

"Really?" said the Grablet with great disinterest.

"Listen to this:

What catches Fly's eye,
Is a parsnip pie."

"Call that a poem?" sneered the Grablet.

Fly tried again. "Here's a longer one:

If you want to fight a Flizzard,
Don't invite it home for tea,
Don't kick it in the gizzard,
Just bonk it on the knee."

"Terrible!" groaned the Grablet. "Spare me any more of this, Danni. Get on with the business please."

Webbers had already taken out the jar and unscrewed

the lid. "Pick a flower, Danni, and you'd better add some of the stem too."

Danni selected a perfect bloom. "If I have to gulp everything down at once, I'd better pull off the petals and break up the stem." To the dash of purple water from the place of mattresses; the fresh and tender leaf from Bearakha; the juice of the ripe, brown cube from Sifania; and the pinch of moondust from Doublesun, she added pink rose petals and pieces of stem from the swamp-rose of Zubel.

Webbers screwed the lid on tight and held the jar out to Danni. "Give it a good shake," he said. "It's taken us on many adventures, but here is your completed Cure, at last. Drink it down, Danni, and say goodbye to the mould forever."

"Thanks Webbers. And thanks to you, Grablet, for remembering the Cure Song," said Danni, reaching happily for the jar.

She never touched it.

The Grablet suddenly zoomed out of Gwenda's hand and socked Webbers in the eye. Webbers staggered. The Grablet dropped to the mud. Danni's fingers missed the jar.

"*Oof!*" went Gwenda as a thrashing tail walloped her in the back a second time.

"*Erka!*" went Fly as a flailing flipper knocked him to his knees.

"*Yaa . . . aaa . . . aaaah!*" went Gwenda, as she was despatched into the swamp by another flick from an uncaring tail.

And Danni?

Danni found herself being smothered in scaly kisses by a thin and bedraggled, very tired-looking Moldy Flizzard.

"Mimi mimi mi mi mimi," croaked the Moldy Flizzard, just managing to *crark* out an exhausted grin. It wasn't the vigorous Moldy Flizzard Danni had first met in her duckpen. The Flizzard's scales were as dry as dog biscuits.

Its wings made a harsh crackling sound as they folded behind its great back. The Moldy Flizzard teetered wearily; it could barely keep on its feet.

But the creature had just enough strength to lovingly hug Danni to its much diminished chest. And just enough to sniff blissfully at her mouldy leg.

For a moment, Danni was stunned, but she came to her senses in a hurry. "No! You can't . . . I haven't drunk the cure yet. Please . . . just let me . . . NO, DON'T! I WON'T GO IN THERE! I WON'T! I WON'T!"

The Moldy Flizzard's pouch had flopped open. It was waiting for her, leering at her.

"Webbers! Give me the jar . . . my cure . . . please . . . !"

The Moldy Flizzard's six-toed feet were sliding backwards towards the swamp.

"Webbers! Quickly . . . quick . . .!"

Webbers looked dazed. He rubbed his eye. He lurched forward, waving the jar. At the same time, the Moldy Flizzard struggled to stay on the bank of the swamp. Its pointy snout jerked up and *Thwacka!* hit the bottom of the precious jar.

The jar rocketed out of Webbers' hand and went sailing into the air. Up, up, higher than the rose tree of Zubel.

Ponderously slipping backwards, the Moldy Flizzard watched the jar.

Crouched on his knees, Fly watched the jar.

Out of one eye, Webbers watched the jar.

Floundering in the swamp, Gwenda watched the jar.

Half-buried in Zubel mud, the Grablet watched the jar.

And, from the Flizzard's arms, Danni watched the jar. Her cure, once almost in her hands, was now out of reach.

The jar rose as high as it could go, and then dropped. Faster and faster, tumbling over and over. Danni knew if it fell in the murky swamp, the jar would be lost forever. She would never find it again. Never!

Skerlop! the jar disappeared. But not into the swamp.

"The pouch!" screamed Danni. "It's gone in the pouch!"

The Moldy Flizzard made another feeble effort to stay on its feet, but its strength was gone. With an almighty splash, the creature toppled backwards into the swamp, where it stuck fast to the bottom.

Danni was stranded on a little island of Flizzard belly. On one side of the island, separated by swamp, was a Flizzard snout, pointing upward. On the other were two Flizzard feet, also pointing upward.

She stood on her belly island and stared at the pouch. It was closed now, and looked like a wrinkled lip. Her priceless Cure, the Cure they had travelled so far and gone through so much to get, was in there. Inside that squelchy pouch.

Danni looked at her mouldy, fungus-flowered leg, and shuddered. It smelled so terrible, she thought she could actually *see* the smell, like a deadly mist. That same foul mould would soon cover every part of her. Even her face!

There was no question about it. She had to get the jar. And she had to get it now, before the Moldy Flizzard revived in its home swamp. But the jar was in the pouch! The only way to get it was . . .

I can't, she thought. I just can't go in that pouch! Desperately, she looked across at Webbers, standing on the edge of the swamp with Fly. Gwenda, who had had to swim for dear life to avoid being drowned by the falling Flizzard, was pulling herself out by using Fly's nose.

Danni opened her mouth to call out to them. But she knew she couldn't do it. "I can't expect any of them to go in the pouch for me," she whispered. "And the Grablet would never go in there. Even if it did, it couldn't carry a jar." Her feet tapped nervously on the Flizzard's belly. "It was me who broke the egg in the first place. It's . . . it's up to me to get the jar out myself." She knelt and lifted the lip of the pouch.

This is the worst moment of my life, thought Danni, gulping a last breath of Zubel air. She closed her eyes, held her nose and dived head-first into the pouch. It welcomed her body with a warm, lapping embrace. Deeper into the dark wetness she slithered, her one searching hand blindly wriggling here and there, seeking the jar.

Would she ever be able to find it? The pouch was so big. The jar was so small. She heard a throb, throb. It's my heart, in my ears! How long can I hold my breath? Where *is* that jar?

Her lungs were bursting; she couldn't hold her breath any longer. As slowly as she could, she breathed out, while her hand fumbled frantically to the left, to the right. I'll never find it! I must have been stupid to think I could! The pouch is enormous. Can't take any more . . . I have to get out . . . now.

Her fingers lightly brushed against something hard. Could it really be the jar? Danni grabbed it anyway. She let go of her nose. Clawing with one hand, rabbit-kicking with both legs, she burst backwards out of the pouch.

As soon as her head was free, she sucked in a breath of life-giving air. Then she drew out her hand. In it was the jar!

Cheers echoed over the swamp. Danni looked up to see Fly and Gwenda rowing their boat towards her. With them was Webbers, standing up and holding the Grablet.

Danni grinned and waved the jar in triumph.

"Swallow it Danni!" urged Webbers. "Swallow! Swallow!"

She unscrewed the lid and gulped the contents. "Not bad," she said. "Tastes like currant jam."

Webbers pulled her into the boat. "I'm proud of you," he said. "Really proud!"

"Brave girl to get in that pouch," said Fly, rowing away from the Flizzard.

Danni rinsed out the jar and returned it to Webbers.

Her cure was now in her tummy and not lost forever in the swamp. She felt very happy about that. Yet, as they rowed away, her face grew smaller and sadder. "Did you notice how thin the Moldy Flizzard was?" she said. "It looked half-starved."

"Skinniest Moldy Flizzard I've ever seen," said Fly, "and Gwenda and I have seen lots. It's only half the size of the dead Flizzard we buried just before we came upon you. Flizzards can grieve to death, you know."

Guiltily, Danni looked back over her shoulder. The Moldy Flizzard wasn't moving. "Do you mean my Moldy Flizzard will die of a broken heart because it's lost its egg? Is that how the Flizzard you just buried died?"

Fly shook his silver curls. "No. Must have been old age, or something else. The egg was still beside the mother, looking very healthy."

"In fact," added Gwenda, "the egg is still there, unburied. We didn't touch it, of course. Who wants a mould?" And she looked pointedly at Danni's leg.

"Not me!" cried Fly. He cleared his throat. "Listen to this:

*I do not think,
I want to stink.*"

"I'd give up all thought of being a poet if I were you," said the Grablet.

"I won't be smelling like a Flizzard's egg much longer," Danni said quietly. "The mould is going. I can see my big toe again. Look, it's just beautiful!"

Webbers bent over for a closer look and even Fly and Gwenda paused in their rowing to inspect her toe.

"The mould is shrinking away from your other toes too," said Webbers. "And the fungus flowers are shrivelling up!"

Forgetting she was in a boat, Danni hopped around, shouting. "It works! The Cure works! I won't be mouldy any longer! It works!"

"That's terrific!" said the Grablet. It sighed loudly. "And now I'm stonkered. Absolutely and totally stonkered. Put me in your pocket for a snooze Danni, and please sit down! I don't want to be lost in this swamp right at the end of our journey."

Danni tucked the Grablet away and sat on Webbers' knee. Her greatest worry was over, but she couldn't get her mind off the Flizzard. "I wonder how long the Moldy Flizzard will need to soak in the swamp," she murmured. "It was so dry it crackled, poor thing. When it comes out, it will have to understand that it has definitely lost its beloved egg for good and all." She sighed as loudly as the Grablet had done. "It's all so terribly sad! And there's an orphan egg here which has lost its mother. That's sad too. It seems . . ." She stopped, and her eyes suddenly sparkled. "Webbers! Couldn't my Moldy Flizzard take the orphan egg and bring it up as her own?"

"No!" said Webbers, Fly and Gwenda together.

"The Moldy Flizzard will only accept its own egg, with its special smell," explained Webbers. "That's why the poor creature has been following you, remember? You have that special smell."

"Of course. I forgot." Danni looked at the mould, disappearing so rapidly that her leg was now bare to the knee. "What if I scraped off a bit of this mould while I still have some, and smeared it on the orphan egg?"

"What? I don't know if it's ever been tried before . . . but . . . it's an interesting idea . . ."

"Let's try! Please Webbers," begged Danni.

"How far away is the orphan egg?"

"Just upswamp from here," said Fly eagerly. "I think it's a great idea!"

"You know, the more I think about it, the more I believe it might work," said Webbers, beginning to look excited.

"Come on, Gwenda!" cried Fly. "Row! Row!" And they

turned the prow of the boat and rowed as hard as they could.

"Faster!" urged Danni. "You'll have to go faster! There's not much mould left!"

20

FINAL
FAREWELLS

They swept around a bend in the swamp and came upon a mighty mound.

"That's it!" puffed Gwenda. "That's where we buried the dead Flizzard. The egg is on the other side."

Rounding the mound, they saw an egg, dripping with mould and sprouting fungus flowers, just like the one Danni had broken.

The boat nosed into the bank and Danni jumped ashore and ran up to the egg. It smelled appalling, but more like rotting fish than the dirty gutter smell she was used to. She glanced at her leg — about three square centimetres of mould remained on her thigh. "I need something to scrape it off with," she shouted. "Quick! Before it goes!"

Webbers was searching a pocket. For once, he found what he wanted straight away. He thrust a wooden lollipop stick into Danni's hand. Very carefully, Danni scraped off the last of the mould onto the end of the stick. There wasn't much more than a speck.

"Watch yourself, Danni," warned Webbers. "Don't let any part of you touch that egg!"

"Don't worry Webbers, I'm not as silly as I used to be." Holding the stick at the very opposite end from the mould, Danni squatted and spread the speck on the top of a fungus flower. "Everyone keep their fingers crossed that this will work," she instructed.

"I would, if I had any," said her pocket.

"You don't smell any more," said Gwenda when Danni was standing next to her again.

There wasn't a trace of mould left on Danni. She rolled up the leg of her shorts a little and laughed. "All gone! See . . . it's all gone, every bit of it!"

Fly peered at the egg, his plaited nose dangerously close to the lush fungus flowers. "Do you think Danni's mould has taken?" he asked.

"It might take to your nose, if you get any closer," said Webbers. "Anyway, we'll soon find out. Look!"

They had all been too intent on what Danni was doing to take much notice of the surging going on in the swamp. Dripping like a warmed-up iceberg, the Moldy Flizzard was splosh, sploshing towards them.

Danni got ready to run. Then she remembered her mould was all gone. What was there to worry about? Also, she was desperately keen to find out what would happen when the Moldy Flizzard saw the egg. Everyone else was interested too. Fly and Gwenda climbed on the grave of the dead Flizzard to get a good view. Webbers followed them. Even the Grablet coughed from Danni's pocket. "I'd like to see if the Moldy Flizzard takes to the . . . er . . . cream puff," it said.

"What?"

"Cream puff . . . oh, sorry, I mean egg."

"You really are tired, aren't you?" said Danni. "Come on then, out you come. We'll join the others on the mound." They all watched as the Moldy Flizzard splashed out of the swamp and stood on the bank, up to its ankles in mud.

"Look at that nice eggy over there!" encouraged Fly. "There's a lovely present for you, Mrs Flizzard."

But the Moldy Flizzard didn't see the egg. It saw Danni and smiled.

"Oh no. Not again!" groaned Danni. Standing on the mound, she was level with the Flizzard's chest, and the creature didn't even have to bend. It easily plucked her off the mound, lifted her up and sniffed her all over.

Snuffle, snuffle, went the pointy snout. *Snuffle, snuffle, sniff, sniff*. "Mimi? Mimi?" said the Flizzard. It sniffed Danni all over again, even turning her upside down to smell the soles of her muddy sandals.

"Whoops! Watch out for the donkeys!" cried the Grablet.

"What?"

"The . . . um . . ."

The Moldy Flizzard gave one last disappointed sniff. Its smile disappeared and its head sagged pathetically. "Whooo . . . oooo . . . ooo," it lamented.

Bitter, amber tears gushed from under the Flizzard's double eyelids and as they gushed, the creature grew weaker and weaker. It seemed the Moldy Flizzard's very life-blood was ebbing away. Danni slipped from its embrace and dropped to the muddy bank.

The Moldy Flizzard swayed from side to side and half-heartedly beat its chest. *Bu-boom! Bu-boom!*

Scooting away from its great legs, Danni stood over the orphan egg. She waved the Grablet around and shouted at the top of her lungs. *"Look, Flizzard! Here's a perfectly lovely egg, just waiting for you. Don't cry, Flizzard! Just look at this egg. It's all yours to love and care for!"*

"Whooo, whooo, whooo . . . oooo," grieved the Flizzard.

"I feel so odd," whispered the Grablet. "Have I got my trousers on?"

"What? No jokes now Grablet, please," said Danni. "Come over here, Moldy Flizzard," she begged. "Please come over here. Why don't you just have a sniff of this egg? It's just as lonely as you are." She flapped her arms to attract the Flizzard's attention. She stamped her feet. "OVER HERE! PLEASE LOOK!"

At last, the Moldy Flizzard looked, holding its neck

in a funny sideways V-shape. Danni watched closely. Were the Flizzard's tears gushing a little less like a waterfall? "Mimi, mimi mi mi mimi," she called, repeatedly jabbing her hand towards the egg. "Mimi, mimi, mimi!"

The Moldy Flizzard flicked at its face with a flipper.

"The suspense of it all! I can hardly bear it!" cried Fly. He dug his nails into Gwenda's arm and trod on Webbers' left web.

Scales creaking, the Moldy Flizzard bent in slow motion. All the way down, a few centimetres at a time. Blinking rapidly, it stared at the orphan egg for at least ten minutes.

Everyone stared at the Moldy Flizzard. Everyone held their breath. Only the Grablet made any noise. It babbled some nonsense about pineapple fritters, so Danni dropped it in her pocket again. She sucked her bottom lip and waited. Fly, Webbers and Gwenda waited.

But the Moldy Flizzard straightened up again. It looked puzzled.

Danni roared with disappointment. "MIMI!" she yelled. "That's Mimi there, you *silly* Moldy Flizzard!"

Even slower than before, the Moldy Flizzard creaked down again. This time, it sniffed the egg.

Please let some of her own mould smell be on the egg, prayed Danni. Please, please, please! She squinted at the fungus flower where she'd smeared the speck, but it didn't look any different from the others.

The Moldy Flizzard sniffed and snuffled over the whole length of the egg. Then it did it again, from end to end. Still bent over, it swivelled its snaky neck and looked Danni straight in the eye. For the second time only, Danni saw the Flizzard's crystal clear, spring-lettuce eyes.

"Mimi?" asked the Flizzard, "Mimi?"

Danni nodded so hard her head nearly fell off. "Yes! Yes! That's Mimi!"

A crafty expression crept into the Moldy Flizzard's eyes

just before the double eyelids hid them once more. "MIMI," it said boldly. Then again, "MIMI."

"That's right," agreed Danni, nodding like a lunatic. "That's your Mimi."

"Mimi, mimi mi mi mimi," shrilled the Flizzard. The smile came back, bigger and longer than ever. The Moldy Flizzard's flippers fluttered over the precious egg like two graceful manta rays. And ever so gently, she picked up the egg and clasped it to her swelling breast. She rocked it like a baby, trilling, clucking, crooning a lullaby.

"Wowee! She's accepted the egg!" bawled Fly. He shook hands with Webbers and went to kiss Gwenda, but poked her in the eye with his nose instead.

Tears she didn't know she was crying tumbled down Danni's cheeks. "G . . . Grablet," she sobbed. "The Moldy Flizzard is treating the egg just like her own. She looks so happy. Now she's taking it away. Isn't it wonderful?"

But there was no reply from her pocket.

Webbers came down from the mound and watched with Danni as the Moldy Flizzard plodded away up the bank, crooning to the egg. Never for a moment did it take its attention from the beloved bundle, not even for one backward glance at Danni.

"She's forgotten all about me, thank goodness," sighed Danni.

"Your idea worked," said Webbers, taking out his comb and mirror. "You've made her happy again. Now we can all go home in peace."

Fly and Gwenda were doing a sort of war dance on top of the mound. It was raining, and Fly had to put his hand over his upturned nostrils.

"That's going to be a problem for Fly," said Webbers. "I expect they get a lot of rain on Zubel. I had a NITT thing somewhere which might help." He rummaged in four pockets and came up with a knitted object, like half an apricot. "This is called a Helpful Heel Hugger but I don't see why it couldn't work as a nose cover instead." He tossed it up to Fly. "Try that. Put it over your nostrils like a cap — it'll stick there by suction."

Gwenda giggled when she saw Fly's plaited nose with the Heel Hugger on the end, but Fly was very happy with it. He came down from the mound and peered in Webbers' mirror, saying:

> *Without a doubt*
> *It looks good on my snout.*

Danni listened for the Grablet's groan, but again there was silence from her pocket. "The Grablet's gone peculiar," she said.

"How?" asked Webbers.

"Well, it called the egg a cream puff and it said something about donkeys and trousers and pineapple fritters. And now it's not saying anything at all."

"It hasn't gone peculiar. It just needs to be recharged."

"What does that mean?"

"The Grablet needs the special electrical currents it can only get on its own planet. It needs recharging, like a battery; to lie and rest and listen to the music of the universe and build up energy again."

Danni shivered. "Surely it doesn't want to go back to that cold old rocky place again? Why can't it come home with me?"

"The Grablet loves that place just as you love Earth and I love Lex," replied Webbers. They moved under a tree to shelter from the rain, and Webbers stretched. "There's such a long way to go, I'll just have a short rest and then we'll be off Danni."

As Webbers slept, Danni stood and looked at him closer than she'd ever looked before. Until now, she hadn't given a thought to parting from Webbers. He had saved her from the Moldy Flizzard and they had travelled so far together. She knew she'd never find another friend like him. She didn't *want* to say goodbye!

It was still raining and Danni was still staring forlornly at Webbers when he woke up. She stirred some mud with her toe. "I'll miss you so much Webbers."

Webbers' smile was soft and tender. "And I'll miss you too, but this is the end of our time together." He brought his NITT notes up to date while Danni said goodbye to Fly and Gwenda.

"Come back and visit us some time," said Gwenda, "but not with a smelly mould please."

"I'll never touch a Moldy Flizzard's egg again, that's for sure," promised Danni. She swallowed the yellow Mos tablet Webbers gave her and pinned down her pocket with one of Webbers' needles, so the Grablet wouldn't fall out while they travelled through space.

Webbers took his deep breaths and, with Danni hanging on behind, left the yellow mud to Fly, Gwenda and the Moldy Flizzards of Zubel.

Danni found it lonely not having the Grablet to chat to. Three times she tried to start a conversation and she even sang a couple of songs all the way through, but the Grablet didn't join in. She couldn't talk to Webbers because he had all his deep breathing to do, so she spent the time thinking about their adventures while they were collecting things for her Cure.

For the last time, Danni landed on the Grablet's planet. It was just as cold and forbidding as she remembered and she wondered again how any being – least of all the chatty Grablet – could put up with such a lonely, gloomy place.

With a trembling hand, Danni unpinned her pocket and took out the Grablet. It felt very cool and all its holes were closed. She pressed it to her lips before laying it next to a craggy boulder. There were all sorts of things she wanted to say to the Grablet but there was an enormous lump in her throat and she didn't know if the Grablet could hear her anyway.

"Ah . . . ah . . ."

For an instant, Danni's heart lept. Was that the Grablet sighing? She bent over eagerly, straining her ears for the slightest word.

"I'm h . . . home . . . ah . . . you know . . .?"

"Yes Grablet? What was that, Grablet? What were you going to say?"

But the Grablet didn't finish.

"Oh Grablet," said Danni in a strange, cracked voice, "if you can hear me, I just want to say you've been the greatest friend. If you hadn't remembered the Cure Song I would have been covered in mould for the rest of my life. I'll never forget you. Goodbye, dear Grablet."

Very faintly, she thought she heard: "Daaannnneeeeeeeee . . ." but perhaps it was only the wind whispering around the crags. With numb fingers, she held onto Webbers' shoulder loops again and they departed the chilly, barren home of the rare Grablet.

Danni tried to stay awake for her last ride through space, but an irresistible feeling of tiredness swept over her and she slept soundly. She did not waken until the blue ball of Earth was beneath her, growing larger and larger. Soon she could make out land, then fields, then her very own duckpen below and, in the blinking of an eye, she was there herself.

It was hard to believe she'd ever been away. The smashed gate still hung on one hinge and the ducks were gobbling in the garden. The footprints of the Moldy Flizzard could be seen around the pond. The lilies lay smashed on their sides.

Webbers bent and pressed Danni's forehead to his cheek. "Goodbye, my dear friend and fellow traveller."

She tried to thank him but when she opened her mouth nothing came out. Only a single tear slid down her cheek. It took just a second to wipe it away, but when Danni looked again Webbers had gone.